WHISPERS IN THE DARK

VOLUME ONE

KALISTA NEITH

<u>**Of Chaos and Darkness Series**</u>

Invoking the Blood
A Trial of Lace and Bone
Whispers in the Dark Vol. 1
(twelve short stories best savored after devouring Invoking the Blood and
A Trial of Lace and Bone)

<u>**Stand Alone**</u>

Soul Obsession (2025)

First published in the United States of America in January 2024 by Ammewnition Studios LLC
www.kalistaneith.com

ISBN 978-1-957303-11-6 (ebook)

ISBN 978-1-957303-13-0 (hardback)

ISBN 978-1-957303-15-4 (paperback)

Book cover and case cover case art by Zoe Holland
Character art by Tonyviento and Zoe Holland

To be kept up with all things in the realms of Chaos and Darkness please visit www.kalistaneith.com and sign up for our newsletter.

Have you ever wanted to follow the characters when they walk off the page and watch them fuck?

This book is for your voyeuristic ass.

Trigger Warnings
(or shopping list)

Contains **SPOILERS** for
Invoking the Blood and *A Trial of Lace and Bone*

- Blood
- Sexual Themes Throughout
- Sexually Explicit Scenes
- Vampires
- Wing Play
- Breath Play
- Rope
- Voyeurism
- Bondage
- Shadow Magic
- Hunter/Prey
- Group Activities
- Exhibitionism

The Realms of Chaos and Darkness

Artithia

A series of floating continents serving as the capital of the five realms.

Necromia

Home to those both the immortal and short-lived who carry soul shards.

Anaria

Referred to as the commoner's lands, this realm is considered a territory of Necromia. Home to the short-lived who do not carry soul shards called Anarians.

Hell

A closed realm containing the souls who have yet to return to the Darkness.

Chaos

The mysterious realm of the Familiar, keepers and caretakers of Chaos and Fate.

Soul Shards

A small marquise cut crystal worn as jewelry, serving as an exterior indication of the power housed within an individual.

Day-Blood
The weaker of the soul shards, indicated by the white tendrils within the clear to grey mist surrounding the soul shard.

Dark-Blood
The stronger of the soul shards, indicated by the black tendrils within the gray to black mist surrounding the soul shard.

Shard of Darkness
A rare soul shard unmatched in strength, indicated when the black mist obscures the soul shard within it.

KALISTA NEITH

WHISPERS IN THE DARK

VOLUME ONE

AMMEWNITION STUDIOS

ARTITHIA • ANARIA • NECROMIA • HELL • CHAOS

SADI
&
DAMIAN

A Night in Bedlam

Fate hadn't always been kind. Damian's lips swept up in a grin. But he would have happily endured his life and worse if he'd known it would lead him to the dark-haired woman strolling beside him. He'd never dreamed Sadi Benevolence, the Familiar Princess, would look his way. She'd found him drowning his anger in a dive bar on the outskirts of Necromia.

She'd turned his barstool and aggressively wedged her hips between his knees, knocking his whiskey glass out of his hand. Her lips met his, and she'd whispered, "I need you…" Damian had been on the verge of telling her she could have him *after* she sobered up when she breathed, "To survive what's coming."

Damian didn't care if she was impaired by spirits or visions. Gorgeous as she was, he didn't take drunk doves to his bed. He'd watched over her that night, and to his disbelief, she'd stayed. He'd gone from banishment from The Order who created him to a resident of Chaos at Sadi's side in less than two years. Most recently, he'd taken his place within the Queen's circle of the Court of Chaos and Darkness.

His life was truly charmed.

He walked through the streets of Bedlam. Chaos's capital wasn't unlike other major cities in Necromia, aside from the building's exteriors changing each time they visited. Shops lined the cobblestone roads while the scent of candied pork and spiced meats wafted from the street merchants.

Sadi purred as she leaned into him and he kissed her temple, inhaling deeply. Her scent of black calla lilies and sunlight soothed him like nothing else. She hooked his teal scarf with a finger and stepped in front of him toward a small man working over a grill. The material tightened around his neck before slipping from Sadi's hold.

Damian loosened the thin cotton and arranged his scarf as Sadi ordered. "Sweet choice cuts, please." She lightly scratched her nails over his bare chest and looked up at him. "Did you want anything?"

An arrogant grin spread across his mouth, and Damian's gaze lowered to the corseted lace she wore. He traced the seam over the tops of her high breasts. "You're the only thing I want to dine on."

She dragged the point of her articulated ring along his jaw and hummed. "You'll have your chance at the festival."

The first time she'd asked him to accompany her to a festival, he'd thought she meant a fairground with music, performers, and games. He quickly learned that although music was enjoyed at Familiar festivals, the performers and games were of a… completely different variety.

Damian was technically a Familiar, but not. He'd been magically bred and raised in Necromia. Honed into a weapon The Order deemed too sharp. He'd never set foot in Chaos before Sadi, but she'd been kind, teaching him Familiar customs. Never faulting his ignorance.

Damian paid three silver marks as his kitten picked up a skewer of sugar-glazed beef and stepped back into the crowd. Thunder crashed as arcs of lightning streaked across the darkened sky, casting its harsh light over the Familiar crowd dressed in various fashions.

The men wore low-slung leather pants, trenches, and colorful scarves to match the make-up dusting their eyes. Damian smiled, recalling Sadi's expression when she woke after spending her first night with him and realized he didn't practice the Familiar custom. She'd surrounded him with pigments in tiny matte jars. A soft brush swept over his eyelids as he blinked up at her. Eventually he learned to do his own eyes, preferring smoke and silvers.

The Familiar doves surrounding them wore complicated outfits aligned with their tastes. The only commonality they shared were tall, belted boots and a corset. Damian glanced at Sadi and smiled as she took dainty bites of her skewer. As lovely as the women surrounding them were in their own way, none of them compared to his kitten.

She held his heart, his devotion, and his will.

They walked with the crowd toward a four-story building. Today, it was a towering brick mansion with turrets and arching peaks. The large picture windows framed inky blackness, as though the turbulent sky above them wasn't enough to constantly remind him he stood in Morbid's realm.

Damian climbed the steps and opened the heavy bloodroot door. Sadi brushed against him as she stepped into the narrow foyer. A dark-haired footman opened the iron gate at the end of the hall-way as they approached.

"Is my father here?" Sadi asked.

"No, Princess," the footman answered.

"Bar his entry if he or my mother visits while I'm here."

"Of course." The footman nodded, and Sadi stepped through the gate into the expansive ground floor the Familiar called *festival.*

The space was spelled, keeping the hall silent, but once Damian stepped over the onyx threshold, moans and screams of pleasure filled the room. Tall candelabras defined spaces for four post beds, X-frames, and other pieces of furniture. When the candelabras were lit, the space was occupied, and additional participants needed an invitation to join. Chaises and chairs surrounded each display, and above them, lining the walls, were three stories of private rooms with balconies overlooking the grounds.

The rooms were similar to the reserved seating found in Nec-romia and Artithia, but royal blood or a noble house didn't afford special treatment in Chaos. These coveted rooms were reserved for those who served Chaos and worshiped fate. A concept daunting even to the Familiar—marked by the numerous unoccupied suites.

Couples and groups occupied several of the spaces. A woman

was strapped to an X-frame with a man kneeling before her. She trembled as he worshipped at her altar, stretching her to take a large toy. In the space beside them, a man was bound to a post. Sweat glistened over his skin as he pulled against his restraints, moaning while his lover fucked his ass.

Sadi tossed her skewer in a bin and dusted her hands, looking around. "Do you want to go upstairs, or should we invite others?"

Sadi's room contained the same furnishings strewn through the festival grounds, but they hadn't picked partners for each other in more than a week. His sweet kitten would be starved for a male or two to join them.

"I think you'd like to ride two cocks," Damian teased. When she glanced up at him inquisitively, he added, "Or did you want a cunt to tongue?"

Sadi dragged the claw of her articulated ring over her bottom lip. "Male today," she answered before arching a brow. "And you, my sweet? Who will you be fucking?"

He asked for a male the last time. "Female, maybe a pair."

"I chose last time. Your pick," Sadi said.

They strolled through the different couples and their crowd of spectators, but their destination was a bit further. A large four-post bed draped in light gray silk remained unoccupied. The candelabras flared to life with a flicker of Damian's mind. He lifted a high-backed leather chair without arms, placing it beside the bed and took a seat. He glanced up at Sadi, patting his thigh.

Sadi swept the train of her skirt over him, and the tulle and lace cascaded over the side of the chair. He clasped the front of her throat, and she lifted her chin, smiling as her back pressed against him. He lazily slid two fingers up her thigh, beginning at her knee. "Who does your cunt belong to?" he asked politely, brushing the side of his face against her soft dark hair.

"You, Damian," she breathed, spreading her legs.

His hand slid higher, caressing her inner thigh. "Such a well-behaved whore for me, kitten," Damian said, searching the crowd as his fingertips trailed beneath her skirt. "Are you wet?" Damian asked, knowing the answer. He scented her arousal while they were outside. His kitten rolled her hips when he softly brushed the back of his fingers over her sex. He squeezed the sides of her throat and pulled her tighter against him.

"Be still, or I'll leave your pussy aching tonight," Damian purred, pressing into her just far enough to give her a taste.

She went still, making a small sound of agreement. Darkness, she was always so wet and responsive. So powerful and yet submissive.

To him anyway, he mused.

Damian circled his thumb over her clit and teased the first joint of two fingers into her cunt. Letting her feel the pleasure of being stretched without the satisfaction of being filled.

Her breaths grew shorter as her chest rose and fell with her moans. Damian nipped the top of her ear, scanning the crowd. Part of his training had been reading people, and he recognized the way Sadi looked at the Shadow Prince. Rune, while powerful, was completely inept with women. If he'd been offered the same opportunity, he would have fucked Sadi thoroughly and often—centuries ago. He would have asked Rune to join their bed, but he was eating out of Faye's hand by the time Damian made his acquaintance and sharing didn't seem high on the little mortal's tenets.

Damian shared and found pleasure in Sadi's ecstasy. He sought out partners for her who resembled the Shadow Prince in some way. Fair hair. Blue eyes. His gaze fell to Tempest, a lean Familiar with frost-blonde hair, tinted with a touch of gold. He and his wife Ava joined their bed often. A trusted, attractive choice who knew the boundaries and rules as well as he and Sadi knew theirs.

"Do you want Tempest to lick your pretty clit? Should I invite him to join us?" Damian asked, stroking the length of his fingers into her.

"Yes," Sadi cried, going rigid.

Damian locked eyes with Tempest and lifted his chin. He smiled in greeting and whispered to his wife before gesturing toward them. Ava's crimson eyes gleamed as she brought her hand to her chest. She vanished before materializing in front of them a moment later.

"How are you, my lovelies?" she asked, flouncing her skirt.

Tempest appeared behind her and draped an arm over her shoulder, pulling her back a step. "You are so impatient."

Ava was a Familiar to her very heart. Unrelenting and unapologetic about her desires. She tilted her head up and her dark curls tumbled over her shoulder. Tempest brushed his thumb over her chin, and her lips parted in a half-hearted hiss.

"Did you want to taste her—"

"Yes!" Ava interrupted.

Damian caressed the front of Sadi's throat, thrusting his fingers deeper. She was so wet, tremoring around his touch. Her nails dug into his thigh and Damian lifted his gaze from Ava to her husband. "Tempest."

"Of course, I do," he answered. His voice slipped through Damian's senses like dark smoke. He stepped closer, taking Damian's wrist and drawing it away from the apex of his kitten's thighs. Sadi blinked, flushed with the color of his attention. She watched breathlessly as Tempest took the length of Damian's fingers past his lips. He bit back a groan. The warmth of his mouth and short strokes of his tongue made Damian's cock twitch. After Sadi was thoroughly satisfied, he would see about asking him if he'd like to join Sadi sucking his cock.

Tempest drew back slowly as though he could hear Damian's thoughts. The tall Familiar winked, taking his time as he sucked Sadi's arousal off of Damian's index before moving to the next.

"Darkness," Damian muttered as his lids slid closed. He opened them when Tempest released him.

He grinned, but not for Damian. His steady gaze remained locked with Sadi's. "And what are we doing to you this evening?"

"Whatever Damian wishes," she answered.

There were so many things to do. Positions to hold her in. He hooked her legs with his, spreading them wide. She leaned back against him, and Damian smoothed his palm down her arms before lifting her wrists and placing her hands behind his neck.

"Tempest is going to do wicked things to your clit," Damian purred.

A throaty laugh flowed over Sadi's lips as her hands tangled in his hair. "Will he?"

Damian purred in agreement. "You could try to resist him and keep your orgasm at bay."

"And why would I do that?" Sadi asked, turning her head to one side.

"Because, kitten, after he makes you come… you're going to get on your knees and spread your legs so he can fuck your ass while you choke on my cock." Sadi made an appreciative sound, and Damian ground his hard length against the soft curve of her ass.

He lightly grasped the front of her neck. "Do you want to be stretched by his cock while I fuck your throat?"

Sadi nodded, rocking back against him.

"Words, dove," Tempest said, running the pad of his thumb over her lips.

"Yes," Sadi breathed.

Ava pulled Tempest's ice blue scarf free and waved it at his cobalt trench and leather pants. "Take all of this off." When her husband arched a brow, she sauntered toward him and unfastened his pants. "I'm not letting you two gang up on her," she said, pulling his cock free. "Besides, I like distracting you."

Damian held Sadi closer, amused by their exchange. Their power dynamic was fluid and would change multiple times over the night. He glanced down at the woman he would walk beside for the rest of his days if she'd let him. She was powerful and assertive outside of the bedroom, but she let her guard down with him. Trusted him to carry her worries and burdens so she could let go.

"We should get you out of this dress," Damian muttered against her hair. Sadi got to her feet and turned to face him. She played with his hair, curling the red streaks around her finger. He pulled her closer and made quick work of her corset's front closure. He laid it down beside his chair, and Sadi shrugged out of the dress beneath it, letting it pool at her feet.

Damian turned her waist and guided her onto his lap, while Tempest and Ava arranged their clothing in a neat pile at the head of the bed.

"Spread your legs for me, kitten," Damian purred.

Her obedience sent a thrill through him, and Damian palmed her breast. She lifted her arms, interlacing her fingers behind his neck. Tempest knelt between Sadi's spread thighs and Damian pinched her nipple, slowly applying pressure until she moaned.

"Who does your cunt belong to, kitten?" Damian asked, locking eyes with the Familiar between his woman's legs.

"You," she answered breathlessly as she arched her back. "Only you."

Tempest gave a curt nod. "I remember."

"You're our favorite pair," Ava said as she called a silver tray of colorful glass bottles and strolled up to her husband. Every move she made was meant to seduce, from the sway of her hips to the way she bounced on her toes, calling attention to her full breasts.

She picked up the red flask and poured the clear oil onto her palm, lowering herself beside Tempest. He slid his hands up Sadi's thighs, spreading her legs wider. His frost-blonde hair fell forward as he dipped his head.

Sadi sucked in a breath and fisted her hands, pulling Damian's hair taut. He squeezed her breasts, pinching her nipples harder.

His kitten whimpered, releasing his hair and he relented, tracing circles around her tight peaks to soothe the hurt. Her breaths labored further as Tempest began purring for her.

Ava fisted his cock and stroked him hard. She giggled when his purr stuttered and worked him ruthlessly.

"I'm going to remember this," he growled against Sadi's silken flesh.

Ava nipped his shoulder and smiled sweetly at him. "Oh, I bet you are."

Damian reached forward, slipping two fingers through Sadi's folds. Her arousal coated his fingers and he spread her open, exposing her clit for Tempest's waiting mouth. "Make her come, and when my sweet kitten is sated, we'll do the same to this one," Damian said, cutting a playful glance at Ava.

Sadi tensed as Tempest roughened his purr. Her breaths were measured as Damian lazily pinched and teased her nipples. A flush bloomed over her chest and crept up her neck, but she fought her pleasure strung along a razor's edge, a moment from breaking.

"Finger her ass," Damian said. "She's wet enough."

Sadi shuddered, arching her back. "Damian."

She was so beautiful when she surrendered everything.

"Submit to me," he purred.

Sadi tensed, straining against Damian. He hooked her legs with his, keeping her spread wide. Holding her exposed, while Tempest licked and sucked, purring on her clit. Tempest brushed his fingers over her center, spreading her arousal lower. He withdrew and a clink of glass sounded. Sadi opened her eyes and met his pale blue gaze. Mischief twinkled in his eyes, and he roughened his purr.

Sadi sucked in a breath, tensing harder. Strain and pleasure coiled within her, winding tighter as her pulse raced. Oiled fingers circled the entrance of her ass and Sadi held his stare knowing the end of their game neared. He winked at her and applied firm pressure, easing inside her. Sadi's head fell back, and she sank her nails into Damian's shoulder.

He worked his fingers in and out of her ass and on the third stroke the tension building in her snapped. She screamed as pleasure crashed over her. Through her. She rocked her hips taking him deeper. Needing the mindless euphoria she found writhing between Damian and Tempest. Where her thoughts became blissfully quiet, consumed by the feel of their bodies moving with hers.

Tempest sat back on his heels and Sadi trembled. Her heart pounded in her ears. Echoes of her orgasm crested over her in lulling waves as Damian's strong arms enveloped her, securing her against him. He purred at her ear and brushed the side of his face in her dark hair.

"Time to get on your knees, kitten," Damian said.

Sadi could hear the arrogant grin in his voice, and it brought a smile to her own. She'd felt death shadowing her, intensifying over the decades. Trusting fate, she'd beseeched the Hall of Empty Eyes, seeking a path to survive what was to come.

They lead her to him.

A vicious, deadly male. Completely devoted to her.

She stood and grasped Damian's gray trench, pulling him to his feet. He stepped into her, and a length of his crimson-streaked black hair fell forward. His metallic eyes reminded her of molten silver, gleaming unnaturally against the dusting of smokey black eyeshadow he wore.

"Take this off," Sadi said, tugging his scarf until the slack looped around his neck pulled tight.

Damian shrugged out of his leather trench and turned, tossing it on the chair behind him. He returned to her, pinching her chin to lift her face. "Undo my pants for me," he said, releasing her.

His quicksilver eyes glittered with possession and Sadi ran the point of her articulated claw over his bare chest. She'd decimated armies but went to her knees for him.

Sadi unfastened his belt and undid his pants. He caressed the side of her face as she pulled him free. His mouthwatering cock was thick and veined. Sadi fisted his shaft and callused hands gripped her hips. She purred, lifting her ass for Tempest as she flattened her tongue and swiped it over the head of Damian's cock.

He tasted like smoked whiskey with a hint of salt. Sadi glanced up as she flicked her tongue. His eyes slid closed momentarily and a soft growl reverberated through him. She opened her mouth wider and closed her lips over the head, hollowing her cheeks as she leaned back. When he slipped from her lips, he opened his eyes and met her gaze.

"I said, choke on it," Damian rasped in the hard-edged, seductive tone she loved.

The tenor of his voice and the dominance in his tone made her wet and when she surrendered—he gave her excruciating bliss. She took his cock past her lips and gazed up at him through the curl of her lashes. Callused hands spread her legs further and the blunt tip of Tempest's oiled cock pressed against her ass.

Sadi moaned, drowning in molten silver eyes. Tempest's cock stretched her, and Damian gave no quarter, thrusting into her mouth. His cock pressed into her throat as Tempest rocked forward. His grip tightened, holding her still while he worked his entire length into her ass.

Her thoughts slipped as they fucked her. Pleasure and euphoria crested through her as she lost herself in the feel of them. The crowd gathering around them no longer mattered. The Crumbling, the threats her court faced, even the feel of death closing in on her—it all quieted.

All she knew was the devotion of her silver-eyed male. His touch. His aggression. His unrelenting need to please her.

Damian pulled away, breaking the ecstasy hazing her mind. He nodded at Tempest. "Take her to the bed."

Tempest wrapped a muscular arm under her breasts and stood, bringing her with him. He sat on the edge of the bed and released her. Sadi flattened a hand over his thigh and glanced back at him. The pale-eyed Familiar leaned onto his elbows and tilted his hips. Sadi stifled a moan as his cock pressed in a little deeper.

Ava crawled onto the bed beside her and whispered, "When it's my turn, I want to tongue your cunt while they fuck me." She and Ava shared a laugh and she crawled higher, pushing Tempest's back to the bed. She straddled her husband's face as she giggled. "I'll make do with your mouth for now."

Sadi's humor was cut short as Tempest rocked his hips. Damian smiled and stepped between their spread legs, clasping her neck lightly.

"Who does your cunt belong to?" he asked in a low growl.

"You, Damian," she answered.

"Mine."

The corners of her mouth lifted into a smile as he squeezed the sides of her neck. He pushed her back onto Tempest's chest, pinning her by the throat. Sadi wrapped her legs over his waist as he thrusted into her.

She screamed her pleasure and rocked with each stroke. She needed more, wanted them rougher. "Fuck me," she pleaded, scratching her nails down Damian's chest.

He growled, capturing her wrists in one hand before lifting them over her head. Callused fingers scraped over her breasts next, and Tempest pinched her nipples while the force of Damian's thrusts dragged her up and down his cock.

The male bodies surrounding her tensed and Damian took a brutal rhythm, fucking her harder. Sadi didn't fight the tension building within her, concentrating on the feel of their hard male bodies. It crested, breaking over her as she screamed her release.

Ava followed a moment later and Sadi felt Tempest's cock pulse as he came. Damian's brow pinched as he lowered his forehead to hers, thrusting into her a final time. "Fuck, Sadi," he growled at her lips, breathless from the force of his release.

She felt his length pulse as he emptied himself deep inside her. He released her hands and Sadi stroked his crimson-streaked black hair.

"Satisfied, kitten? Or do you need another go?" Damian asked.

Tempest circled the pads of his thumbs over her nipples, and she sighed. "I think if you don't give Ava her turn, she'll puncture one of your lungs," Sadi said casually.

"I would heal it right after," Ava added.

Damian laughed and nuzzled her throat. "As you command."

MORBID & ANGELIQUE

Takes place during chapter 53 of Invoking the Blood.

Morbid clasped his hand over the Shadow Prince's shoulder and met his gaze. "Every answer you seek lies directly in front of you."

Angelique took priority over the young prince, and he'd kept his wife from Chaos far longer than she cared to tolerate. Morbid phased before Rune could continue his argument and materialized in his bedroom.

Silks and tapestries decorated their walls, but his wife's pride was the polished chandelier, hand-strung with thousands of rubies and diamonds. The coffered ceiling was built specifically for Angelique's trinket, and she stared at it often, for hours at a time.

His wife sank her little fangs into the knuckle of his thumb to show her displeasure and leaped to their bed. Spending the night in Hell put her in a sour mood, but he had every intention of making it up to her.

Morbid shrugged out of his trench and let it fall to the floor. He moved closer, searching for the sleek white cat. She hid between the bunched down blankets strewn over their platform bed. "Don't be angry, kismet," he purred.

A brilliant light flared over the plethora of raw silk. The glow faded to reveal his naked wife, laying on her stomach. He sat beside Angelique and her scent simultaneously aroused and relaxed his senses. She was his orchid on a sea cliffside. Beautiful and strong, yet best kept in an environment suited to her.

He brushed her dark strands away from her face and she hissed at his kindness before turning away. "We were helping Michelle's son," Morbid crooned. He smoothed his hand up the curve of her thigh. "Do you remember Julian and Michelle?"

Angelique perked up immediately and curled onto her side, facing him. Her blue-gray eyes captured the storming skies above his realm, but he was no king here. It was she who ruled him with her cunning eyes and soft curves.

"Is it the new moon?" she asked as her eyes gleamed.

Michelle and Julian were Angelique's favorite pair. In the days of their rule, the new moon had been a standing date between them. They'd spend the evening at a Familiar festival or simply fell into each other's beds.

His queen's mind had become Chaos-touched after the assassination attempt that nearly took her life. Linear history meant little to her, and memories folded into others, bending timelines through her mind.

Angelique asked for Michelle and Julian—without fail—each time the night sky cleared.

"No, it's not the new moon," Morbid said gently.

"I miss them," she said, dragging the clawed point of her articulated ring up the inner seam of his pants.

"I miss them, too," Morbid murmured.

Angelique pulled his belt open and stared up at him through the dark fan of her lashes. "Do you want me to kiss your metal?"

Her eccentricities had his cock hardening in an instant. "You can kiss whatever you like, kismet."

He stood and Angelique tightened her hold on his waistband, hissing loudly. A dark chuckle rolled past his lips, and he tapped the underside of her chin. "I'm not taking your metal from you. You'll be more comfortable if I stand."

Angelique pondered his words and after some consideration, sat back on her heels. She straightened her arms in front of her and crossed her wrists over her thigh. His gaze dipped as she pressed her generous breasts together and leaned to the side, emphasizing the curves he absolutely adored. Her blue-gray eyes lingered on his face before drifting lower to devour his chiseled body.

"Take them off," she commanded.

Morbid slowly tugged on his fuchsia scarf, letting it drag across his neck as it rustled his long black hair. He tossed the gauzy material over her thighs, and she scowled at him.

"You're not funny."

"Life's simple complexities are quite amusing," he said, unfastening his pants. He pulled his cock free, and she purred, inching to the edge of the bed.

"Are you going to fuck me wearing those?" Angelique asked as her gaze swept past his knees.

Morbid grinned. If she'd been in cat form, she would be flicking her tail at him with her ears pinned against her head. "I suppose, I could be moved to appease my wife," he said, kicking off his unlaced boots.

Angelique's nails sank into the raw silk and her eyes took on a predatory glint as he stripped off his leather pants. He stepped into her, catching the top of her throat and squeezed the hinge of her jaw with his thumb and index. "Are you going to suck my cock the way I like, kismet?"

She leaned into his hold and smiled up at him. "Yes."

"Good girl," he purred, sliding his hand to the base of her throat. He called one of their lingerie collars and a strip of supple leather materialized around her neck. She gasped as straps extended from it, weaving over her arms and legs.

Morbid flicked a finger up and Angelique's arms jerked above her head, yanking her to her knees. She moaned as he palmed her breast, dragging the pad of his thumb across her tight nipple.

"Are you going to spread your legs, or am I going to make you?" Morbid asked.

He hissed a breath when she ignored him and licked the tip of his cock. Darkness, no one sucked his cock like she did. The warmth of her mouth. The way she tongued the metal bars under the head.

"Purr for me. Yes. You're such a good girl," Morbid groaned as she took him deeper.

He called a roll of leather the less experienced would believe carried knives. It spilled open with a flicker of his mind. Vials of oil, a variety of phallic appendages, and textured sleeves his wife requested he wear over his cock from time to time were nestled in their compartments. He carried several kits for Angelique, rotating them depending on her mood.

When she was calm his wife preferred soft, textured toys, twisting, and grinding in her pussy and ass. Alternatively, when his wife needed some aggression worked out of her, he happily restrained her and fucked both of her pretty holes. She'd cry out as he mercilessly edged her with his will or stretched and filled her with hard toys. He brought her so close; a well-placed breath would have her screaming his name.

Morbid provided her with anything she desired, and his kismet loved her games. It was delicate and nuanced, spanning centuries. The rules were quite simple. If she managed to make him come in her mouth, she won and he was hers to command, *without question*, for the rest of the day. His queen rarely won and surrendered when she was breathless and spent, sprawled over their sheets—but he would be lying if he said he didn't enjoy her valiant attempts at victory.

He ran his fingers through her dark tress, admiring the streaks of red she recently added. She opened her mouth wider and leaned forward, pressing him into her throat. "Take it all, kismet. Every inch," Morbid grated.

She obeyed and his breath hitched. Darkness, he loved her on her knees. The way she sucked and licked, tonguing his piercings. She stared up at him through teary lashes. Her luscious breasts swaying as she slid up and down his cock.

Three straps hung from Angelique's modified lingerie collar and flowed over her back. He'd spelled each of them to fuck his lovely wife with various toys. They worked alone, or in pairs. He occasionally deployed all three, watching Angelique's pleasure while he licked and teased her nipples.

Two straps tonight, he thought as he picked out a pair of light pink appendages. They were narrow at the tip and tapered to a thick base with baroque patterns, sweeping up their length. His cock was much harder than her toys, but Angelique acquired a taste for their giving density. Morbid poured oil over the two decorative shafts and the leather strips lowered behind her.

"Are we playing tonight, kismet? Or did you want me to fuck you?" he asked.

She pulled away from his cock and glanced up at him. Morbid brushed her throat, rubbing soothing circles over the delicate muscles at the base of her jaw. She was beautiful with her full curves and soft stomach, bewitching his every thought.

"Fuck me," she breathed.

Morbid went to his knees and used the straps laced around her legs to spread her wide. He gave her no quarter, commanding the leather leads to thrust inches of the oiled pink tips into her.

"Morbid," she cried, pulling against her restraints.

"You've been mine for millennia, kismet," he said, gliding his fingertips up her thigh. His touch grew slick with her desire as he gently spread her open. Angelique's breath caught as he idly teased her cunt, relishing the feel of the spelled appendages thrusting past his fingers.

"You should choose your words more carefully…" He leaned closer, tasting his wife's sweet lips as his fingers drifted higher. He pulled back and stared into her stormy eyes as he circled her clit. "Or do you enjoy our specific brand of foreplay?"

Angelique trusted him completely and allowed him free entry into her mind. There was pleasure in the flesh, and he was more than capable of making her come with his body alone. But a Familiar's canvas was the mind and what he commanded; her body obeyed.

He willed the straps to thrust harder, stretching her around the thick base. His wife trembled and Morbid seized her mind, intensifying her pleasure until she felt every raised curve of her toys in her sensitive cunt and ass.

Angelique screamed as she came, desperately pulling against her bonds.

Morbid captured her wrists in one hand and pinned her beneath him. He withdrew her toys but held their sensation in her mind. She would feel them stroking into her while he fucked her. A purr rumbled from his chest as he gazed down at her silken flesh.

"Spread your legs for me, kismet. Wider," he purred, pleased with her obedience.

He thrusted into her wet heat and her inner walls rhythmically squeezed his cock. A fully trained male could hold her orgasm for thirty minutes before his talents ran slim. Morbid was capable of holding her mind here indefinitely and found fucking her while she came pleasant. He was a simple man after all. Heat, friction, and her soft cries of pleasure were all he needed to feel satisfied.

Angelique panted beneath him, taking every stroke.

"You are such a good girl. Spreading your legs and taking all of my cock," Morbid murmured, increasing his pace and taking her harder. He fucked her like this until a thin sheen of perspiration covered her flushed skin and she could no longer form intelligible words.

"Should I come, or would you like your ass fucked, kismet?" Morbid asked between thrusts.

Angelique nodded once and Morbid hooked his arms under her knees. He sat back on his heels, dragging her against him until her ass lifted off the bed. She took his cock in long hard strokes.

Every inch.

Every piercing.

Morbid's back tensed and his breaths became ragged. He buried himself inside her a final time, emptying himself deep inside her.

He released her mind, letting the sensations slip away as he drew her into his arms. She clung to him, resting her head on his shoulder. He gazed down at his fated queen and grinned at the sprinkling of freckles across her flushed cheeks.

"I want to go to a festival," she breathed against the side of his throat.

A brilliant light engulfed her and Morbid adjusted his hold as she shifted into a sleek white cat. He cradled her in the crook of his arm and affectionally stroked the back of her neck.

"Anything you wish, kismet."

ALISTER & PRINIA

BLOOD AND WHISKEY

Takes place during chapter 30 of A Trial of Lace and Bone.

I misjudged her, Alister thought as he considered the woman across the oak sitting table. Rune studied beneath Saith as a child and idolized his psychotic mentor in the same way a boy would his father. The Creator molded his brother into the Shadow Prince, and Rune had been enamored and too shortsighted to see the situation for what it truly was.

His brother was a cruel weapon, wielded by a weak man.

Faye was the first person Rune bowed to since Saith's death. And while the *illustrious* Shadow Prince still carried many of his vicious mentor's prejudices, the young mortal tempered Rune's misguided views.

But Rune had not been the only one led astray.

Alister glanced into his tea. Faye had offered her absolute surrender, however their definitions of absolute differed and his terms did not include Faye's continued existence.

He'd thought to be merciful and decapitate her. When Rune's shield prevented him from providing her with a clean death, he enacted his contingency plan—drowning her in a coffin as vengeance for his brother's cruel deeds against his wife.

Alister tapped his fingers on the table and exhaled, reflecting on the decisions he made in a rage-filled haste. Faye's was the only court in history to offer sanctuary for a love like his, but he'd exiled himself the moment his blade dragged across her slender throat.

"I don't expect you to trust me. I'll have to earn that, and I have every understanding you are only here because of Prin," Alister said while Prinia turned her plate, scrutinizing the almond cookies. She selected one and Alister grinned, savoring the small moment before his attention returned to Faye. "My brother has always held the position of executioner. He has never handled the internal workings of a court. I have."

"He is my consort," Faye said quietly as her fingers tightened around her teacup. Her gold-slashed eyes lifted to meet his. "Why do you want to join a court he is an integral part of?"

Alister's heart hollowed, and he gazed at his wife. Prin's pink-blushed lips parted as she nibbled her cookie. He held his expression, taking note of the diminutive points edging his wife's canines. She would hunger for more than the dessert could offer soon. His sweet Prin had returned different but, in many ways, she was the same. He'd spent centuries begging the Darkness to let her wake, dreaming of the day she would return to him.

Each morning he rose to her clouded eyes silently reminding him she suffered because he loved her.

Alister swallowed thickly before lowering his voice and admitting, "Because if your court existed eight centuries ago, we would have had a place to belong." Faye silently stared at him and he knitted his brows. "Do you truly think I'm the only day-blood to fall in love with an Anarian?"

Prinia pulled her lip over her teeth and licked the top of her mouth. "I think these cookies are bad. They taste funny."

"I'm sorry, sweetheart. I'll go to the market and bring you another tin," Alister said, amending the truth. There was nothing wrong with Prinia's favorite dessert, but she fought her thirst until she was so starved her eyes flooded onyx.

Alister gently took the crumbly yellow cookie, dotted with a red circle at its center, and placed it on the small porcelain dish. Prinia dusted her fingers, pouting to herself.

"I'll need to speak to your brother about it," Faye murmured.

Alister nodded and slid Prinia's tea closer. She ignored her cup and snuck a cookie off her plate, concealing it beneath the table. He'd expected to see humor or mirth in Faye's strange eyes, but an apprehensive stare scrutinized him.

She perceived him as a threat and monitored him exclusively.

Prinia was blissfully indifferent to the silence echoing between himself and Faye. She held the pale almond cookie out and her shadowed hellhound lifted its massive head, gently accepting its master's offering.

"If you allow me to assist the Court of Chaos and Darkness, I will need a space for Prinia *he* cannot enter," Alister volunteered.

His wife's mental state deteriorated at the mention of his brother's name, and thankfully Faye understood Prin's… sensitivity. His wife endured eight hundred years of terror-filled panic, and he would bend the Darkness itself to arrange her happiness for the rest of eternity.

"I understand," Faye answered.

Prinia choked, coughing into her teacup. She recoiled, flicking it away as though her drink had attacked her. Alister caught glass before the thin porcelain cracked against the table.

"It tastes bad," she cried.

Her soft features pinched, and she curled into herself, taking up less space. Alister caressed the underside of her jaw and gently lifted her face. Her dark eyes turned glassy with unshed tears, and Alister's heart bled.

Of all the wars and hard-earned battles he'd fought, all the enemies he'd vanquished, he would trade them all to wipe away his wife's fears as easily as he dabbed the tea from her trembling lips.

Prinia shook her head, turning away from the cloth and crawled onto his lap. Alister lifted her easily and settled her across his thighs, cradled in his arms. "I know, love. It's okay," he murmured, stroking her back. Prinia quieted, fixating on a piece of embroidered lace stitched into the bright blue skirt of her dress.

Alister held her tighter, reminding himself she was real. Returned to him by the young mortal. He inhaled deeply, breathing in Prinia's sweet rose-water scent. He met Faye's scrutinizing gaze with one of his own, determining no clear way to bridge the chasm he'd unearthed between them.

He owed Rune's Queen so much and could never repay his debt.

"I never thanked you for bringing my wife back to me," Alister said more to himself than Faye.

Prin nuzzled his throat and rolled her hips, grinding against his cock. Alister smoothed his hand over her hip beneath Faye's view, holding her still. A purr vibrated from his wife as black swept through her stare and Alister silently cursed in High Tongue.

Faye seemingly recognized his words and stood suddenly, nearly knocking the chair over. She turned her back to them and said in a rush, "I'm going to go, but I'll visit Prinia again."

"Thank you," Alister said as she phased away.

He stifled a groan as Prin pressed her soft lips to the side of his throat. The heat of her mouth lingered on his skin, electrifying his senses. Darkness, he missed her. Fear was his constant companion, lingering at the edges of his mind. Anxiety clawed at him, whispering she would be taken from him. Again. Or this was all an elaborate Familiar fantasy woven through his mind and he would be forced to return to lying beside her still body—silently begging her clouded, milky eyes to clear and meet his.

As they had for centuries.

Before he lost her, Prinia would curl on her side with him when they turned in for the night. Her legs tangled with his while they spoke about their day. She'd been too shy to ask for her pleasure and Alister happily followed her lead, adapting to her silent demands. If she guided his hand to the curve of her hip, he would lean closer and ask, "Do you want me, sweetheart?" She'd flush and give him the tiniest of nods.

"Want you." Prinia's throaty words drew Alister from his memories. She nipped his throat and dragged her tongue over his heavy pulse.

"Have me," he answered as he stood, lifting her into his arms.

She twisted, digging her nails into his shoulder before opening her mouth wide and sinking her fangs deep.

Alister's knees nearly buckled. He hadn't completely acclimated to the changes in his wife. *Darkness save him*, he'd thought he'd known what to expect. He understood a vampire's bite simulated the sensation of sex to placate their prey. He'd been woefully unprepared and completely caught off guard the first time she'd bitten him.

It felt like he was inside of her. The exquisite heat and friction sliding down his cock in a sensual stroke as her canines penetrated his flesh.

Prinia had been timid before she turned—and still was—for the most part. Her revulsion to blood, while ironic, left him with her predatorial side when she was starved, and her dark eyes flooded black with bloodlust.

She craved him for sustenance and pleasure. Alister climbed the stairs to their bedroom, taking the steps three at a time. He reached the top and Prinia released her bite. The feeling over his cock withdrew while she licked his blood from his neck. Alister stifled a groan and Prinia purred happily, lapping the crimson trails streaking his throat.

The soft rumble stopped suddenly. She tore his shirt at the collar and raked her nails over his chest. Blood rose along the red welts and Prinia dipped her head. Her tongue caressed the raised marks she'd left on the hard muscles of his chest. Alister ignored the burn.

His little wife was all too happy to sink her fangs into him, but she wouldn't drink.

Which lead Alister to improvise.

The heels of his boots scraped against the hardwood floor of their bedroom. Prinia wrapped her legs around his lean waist, lifting her head momentarily before sinking her petite fangs into the opposite side of his throat.

Alister shuddered a breath and dropped a knee onto their bed. The blue silk bunched around Prinia's waist, exposing silk stockings tied at the top of her thighs with mismatched ribbons. He untied her corset closure and pulled the strings loose. The gown yawned, falling away from Prinia's slim shoulders and she growled, shoving the material down her arms.

He pulled her closer and lifted his vicious vampire out of her dress. She didn't seem to notice her ballet flats slipped off her feet, lost in the discarded skirt.

Prinia was considerably stronger than she once was. Her nails bit into his back as she flattened her tongue to lick the crimson trails lining either side of his throat. Alister gently stroked her back and she responded with a growl. Her legs constricted around him until he was sure she was bruising her inner thighs on his waist.

Alister lifted his head, offering her his throat as he lowered himself to his knees near the nightstand. He dragged his pillow to the ground and caressed her calf, following the smooth curve of her leg behind him. He forcibly unhooked her ankles and Prin made an exasperated sound, sinking her fangs into his shoulder. She flexed her jaw, biting harder and ecstasy stroked the entirety of his length. Alister stuttered a breath. Darkness, he wanted nothing more than to tear her panties off and bury his cock in her soft cunt.

He untangled himself from her embrace and murmured, "Give me your pretty fangs," as he stood. Her wholly black eyes left no room for illusions.

A predator was taking his measure.

Calculating.

Waiting.

Alister unfastened his belt and Prinia went perfectly still, her blood-starved gaze dipping lower. She licked her blush-stained lips and inched closer. He intercepted her before she crawled off the pillow and ended up bruising her legs on the wooden floor.

Prinia purred, rising on her knees. She yanked on his waistband, jerking him closer.

"Easy, love," Alister said, pulling himself free. He angled his cock near Prin's face and curled his fingers around the lower half of his length.

Prinia's lips brushed the side of his shaft sending vibrations up his cock. She licked the underside of his head and opened her mouth wide, sinking her fangs into the shaft just after the crown.

Pleasure racked Alister, devastating his control. He'd been abstinent during the past eight centuries, and while he had no intention of being unfaithful to his wife, he was woefully out of practice. His wife's new abilities proved to be a violent learning curve.

Phantom warmth and friction slid down his cock and withdrew as Prinia released her bite. Euphoria clouded his thoughts and Alister struggled to maintain control.

Prinia shoved his hand away and fisted the base of his cock. She ran her nails across his waist, drawing blood as she took him into her mouth. Heat encased him and the feigned sensations began anew, moving all the way down his shaft and back as Prin worked a few inches in and out of her mouth.

Alister called his two-handed sword and leaned against it hard, resting his forehead on the pommel. He silently wondered how men withstood this. His sweet wife was going to escort him to the Darkness.

Prinia would bite and refuse to drink but sucked greedily when his cock was in her mouth.

Did it have to feel like he was fucking her throat? Alister thought somewhere between bitterness and bliss.

Prinia had claimed to enjoy oral when she was mortal. Alister remained skeptical, thinking she only did so to please him. But the way she clawed at his waist, greedily swallowing half of his cock in her bloodlust—he was inclined to believe her.

Alister white-knuckled his sword hilt and let Prinia do as she pleased. He stroked her cheek and ran his fingers through her shimmering, fawn colored hair as she purred, sending maddening vibrations up his shaft.

Alister stood his ground until his muscles seized with tension. Prinia might delight in having his cock in her mouth, but she wouldn't appreciate him coming on her tongue.

A preference Alister was certain her bloodlust hadn't altered.

He tossed his sword over the foot of their bed and groaned as she sucked harder, curling her tongue over the tip. Alister caught himself before his legs buckled. He would need to tactically withdraw from the sublime feel of her lips before he came on her tongue, and she bit down on his dick in earnest.

"You need to give that back, sweetheart," Alister rasped as he begrudgingly withdrew from her mouth.

A growl replaced the low thrum of Prinia's purr, and she bared her fangs, hissing, "Mine!"

Alister chuckled as he slid his hand under her jaw, gently holding her at a distance. If she reengaged him on her preferred field, he would lose. Badly.

He lowered himself to her level and took her into his arms, pulling her against him as he rose. "Don't you want my cock in your pussy?" he asked against her hair.

The quiet rumble of her purr sounded again and Alister leaned away, taking in her expression. Her pouting lips were swollen, and a bright pink blush flushed her cheeks. Her vampiric state exaggerated her features, but her dark eyes remained the same.

They were a winter forest he would never hope to escape. Her beauty was a shadowed wisp leading him into her woods but once he stepped through the brush, her gentle soul became his all-consuming muse.

Prinia's thick lashes lowered. *Placated for the time being,* Alister thought. He pulled her in, and their lips met in a soft caress. Prinia frantically deepened their kiss. The metallic taste of blood whispered through his mouth. And while he derived no pleasure from bloodletting, knowing Prinia had writhed while taking his blood and sucking his cock made him impossibly hard. Her nails raked his back and Alister sucked on her tongue, careful to keep her fangs from nicking him.

Prinia pulled away, breaking their kiss. She stared down at him with passion glazed eyes and her attention drifted to his throat. Alister held still as she ran her hand across the crimson trails and smeared the red across the hard muscles of his chest.

Alister quietly ripped Prin's panties while she studied the blood on her hand. She giggled and held his stare as she ran the tip of her tongue from the base of her palm to the end of her middle finger.

"Darkness," Alister muttered, certain she would be the death of him.

Alister sat in the oversized upholstered chair he'd purchased specifically so Prinia could ride him without bruising her shins.

Her fingers closed over the front of his throat, and she rose up on her knees. Her lips curled into a playful smile, and she nipped his bottom lip before hissing, "Mine."

A groan escaped Alister as she lowered herself on his cock. She rolled her hips, taking the head, the heat of her cunt squeezing him as she inched lower. Alister reached for the small table beside the chair, blindly patting his hand over the bloodroot surface. His wedding band clinked against the decanter of whiskey, and he found the thin, articulated gauntlet resting beside it.

He reached behind Prinia, struggling to fasten the elaborate piece of jewelry as she worked herself up and down his length. Alister's breath hitched. She took him deeper with each fall, twisting her hips before lifting off him until the tip of his cock nearly slipped free before lowering onto him again.

Alister's toes curled, and he clenched his jaw as Prin quickened her pace. He lifted his hand over her shoulder to inspect the gauntlet. Small tubes threaded over the thin, articulated bands of silver covering his index and middle finger before spreading to a plate on the back of his hand. It was enchanted to draw from a cache of blood. Typically, this type of jewelry was used for wine or other drinks during intimate play, but Alister supposed crimson wine was still wine.

He slipped two fingers into Prinia's mouth, and she sucked, drinking while she rode him. Her hair bounced with her movements and Alister stared, entranced with the sway of her breasts. He palmed the right and pinched her nipple, eliciting a moan from his wife. She panted around his fingers, quickening her pace.

Allister's eyes slid closed. She felt divine, driving him closer to a blissful release with each rock of her hips.

One he was unable to submit to until her onyx eyes cleared.

He'd learned to prolong her frenzy by coaxing her arousal and manipulating her oral fixation. He silently prayed to the Darkness he could subside her thirst before she rung his ecstasy from him.

Prinia's fingers dug into either side of his throat, tightening until she cut off his airway. He didn't struggle or fight her. Only lifted his chin as he tilted his head back, leaving himself a sliver of breath. He lowered his lashes, tracking each fall of her hips.

Her hair fell forward as she took her pleasure, tumbling in front of her high breasts. Alister pushed the loose strands behind her shoulder. She'd been gentle and shy as a mortal, flushing deeply when he undressed her. He outlined the curve of her breast while she rocked over him. Prin would never have ridden him with such abandon under normal circumstances. He would learn every desire his vampiric wife possessed, just as he had when he began courting her centuries ago.

Alister tugged her nipple, capturing it between his index and middle finger before rubbing the pad of his thumb across his fingertips, teasing the very tip. Prin arched her back, sinking lower on his cock.

"Allie," she moaned around his fingers.

A smile curled his lips, and he continued until the bright pink flush decorating her cheeks traveled down her throat and bloomed between her breasts. Satisfied, he dropped his hand, splaying his fingers at her navel and slipped lower.

"Come for me, sweetheart," Alister rasped through her hold. He circled her clit and she shuddered. "Take all of my cock." Her grip tightened and Prin pitched her head back, riding him harder.

"Good girl," Alister grated. "Take it. All of it."

Her fingers bruised his throat and Prinia rocked her hips once more before going still with a shrill cry. Her cunt squeezed him intimately, and Alister wasn't sure if he'd lost his breath over the exquisite vision of his wife coming around his cock or her hand on his neck.

The black of her eyes wisped for a moment, revealing slivers of white before they were swallowed entirely.

Alister withdrew his hand from her mouth and roughly poured a glass of whiskey. The amber liquid sloshed over the rim and splashed onto the bloodroot surface. He took a deep drink and pulled Prinia into a possessive kiss. His tongue slid over hers as he angled his head, forcing her jaw wider.

He withdrew suddenly and took another swig of the smokey liquid before pillaging her mouth a second time, replacing the bright, metallic taste of blood with the bite of his alcohol.

Prinia's grip on his throat loosened and her hand gently slid down his chest.

"Allie," she whispered, rolling her hips to take his cock in a much gentler rhythm.

She stilled and her gaze wandered from his throat to the crimson smearing his chest, and finally coming to rest on her hands.

"I was painting," Alister crooned, drawing her attention with a thrust of his hips.

"Oh," Prinia sighed. She wrapped her arms around his neck and held him close, hiding her exposed body. "You're very messy when you paint."

"Only because you insist on everything being the same color as your ugly flowers," Alister answered with a grin. He trailed his kisses down the underside of her jaw and palmed her ass when she shuddered.

"Do you want to come again, sweetheart?" Alister asked.

"You make me glitter and float like the stars," she breathed.

Alister held her close and stood, taking her to their bed. He caged her beneath his body and smoothed his hand up the back of her thigh. She crossed her ankles behind him and Alister gently stroked into her wet heat.

Prinia intertwined her fingers with his and moaned, taking him deep.

He brought her hand to his mouth and brushed his lips over her knuckles. "You're my haven," he whispered before lifting his hand over her head. He trapped her palm beneath his, rhythmically pressing her fingers into the comforter with each thrust.

Alister groaned, cherishing her sighs and little moans of pleasure. Each time she gasped his name Alister's chest tightened. Moments he'd thought lost had come back to him.

She had come back to him.

Prinia traced the side of his cheek, and he lifted his head. Her deep brown eyes caught the light burning from a single candle, reflecting flecks of red and burgundy. She stared up at him, blinking as her brow drew together. Her blushed lips parted, and she moaned as he thrusted deeper. He committed every expression—each gesture—to memory. He needed her being branded on his soul.

"Allie," Prin cried in a breathless whisper.

"Are you glittering for me?" Alister asked as he reached between them. He teased her clit and Prinia's thighs tightened over his waist, trying in vain to pull her legs together. "Take it for me, love. Let me in," he rasped, thrusting harder.

Prinia's back bowed off the bed as she panted. She writhed beneath him, tightening the intertwined fingers he'd pinned to their bed.

"Take me deeper," Alister groaned, stretching her until she accepted the last inch of his cock. "You're such a good girl."

Intimate flutters squeezed his length and the tension melted from Prinia's body, leaving her boneless beneath him.

"Give me your stars," she moaned breathlessly between labored breaths.

"Yes, sweetheart," Alister murmured reverently. His arms tightened around her, and he breathed in her rose-water scent. He surrendered to the feel of her. Her palm under his. The warmth of her flushed skin. The way her cunt squeezed his cock with each stroke, begging him to come in her.

She consumed his senses—surrounding him until he couldn't discern the forest from the trees.

Tension built at the base of his spine as burgeoning pressure steadily climbed up his shaft. He didn't resist it, losing himself in Prinia and her gentle touch. He thrusted hard, driving into her a final time. His cock pulsed and he couldn't breathe as he came, emptying himself deep inside of her.

"Your stars make me glitter," Prinia whispered, rolling her hips.

Alister shuddered, catching his breath as pleasure tremored through his body.

She crossed her ankles behind him, drawing him closer. She glided her fingers through his short black hair stared into his eyes. "It feels like I've loved you forever."

Alister smiled and kissed her in answer before promising, "We have forever, and I'll love you for the rest of eternity."

SPARROW & VASHIEN

SUNSHINE

Takes place before Invoking the Blood.

Vashien's rough fingertips tangled through Sparrow's curls, sending electrified tingles through her body before his grip tightened along the base of her neck. The pressure of her hair pulled taut was a kiss of adrenaline. Her skin tingled and she stood on her toes, quietly anticipating what Vash would do next.

Her tall, dark, and winged reached past her, unlocking the over-sized oak door to his loft. He called it theirs for more than two years, but it wasn't really. Faye's stubborn ass wouldn't leave Anaria and Sparrow remained to make sure rogue dark-bloods didn't fuck with her.

Vashien leaned closer and Sparrow's eyes widened. The thoughts of her sister evaporating like morning dew. He spoke softly, coasting his lips over the shell of her ear. Sparrow shivered as he dragged out his words. "You've been a brat all day."

She had, Sparrow thought, her mouth stretching into a wide grin. Teasing him in public was the absolute highlight of her day. A secret game no one else knew they played.

She loved stroking the sensitive spot inside his wings, where the membrane met his back and took advantage of *every* opportunity. The best part? The tension in his body as he drew a sharp breath before capturing her wrist.

It was like sucking his dick in public and getting away with it.

"You wouldn't like me if I was boring," she breathed, reaching behind her. She flattened her hand over the silk of his maroon dress shirt and traced every curve and dip of his muscular body before sliding her fingertips beneath his belt. Her finger curled around the tip of his cock, and the tension on her scalp increased.

"You're asking for it," Vashien growled, shoving the oak door open.

He spun her to face him and gripped the back of her thighs, lifting her against him. She blinked widely, letting her glittering red dress straps slip down her shoulders.

"Fuck me. I've been waiting all night," she said, leaning closer to press her full breasts into his face.

He bunched her dress over her hips, and Sparrow pulled him closer as he squeezed her ass. "Good girls get fucked. Bad girls get punished. And you, Sunshine, have been very bad," he said, rubbing his stubbled chin along her shoulder.

"I'll be good," Sparrow said, wrapping her arms around his neck. "I'll *play nice.*"

His hazel eyes lowered to her crimson-stained lips, and Sparrow smiled. Playing nice wasn't exactly a punishment. She had moods where she wanted to be on her knees, wrists straining against the rope he meticulously tied behind her back, so he could fuck her throat as he pleased.

"I'll play *really* nice, Wing Daddy," Sparrow purred.

Vashien's impressive wings caught her attention three years ago. And if it was one thing Sparrow lacked, it was restraint. Her curiosity got the best of her. She needed to see for herself if the rumors were true. *Did wingspans correlate to dick size?* He'd been so shy and cordial when they first met, she nearly lost interest.

Luckily, he held her attention in other ways. He never told her to behave or calm down during those first few months because she was too much. He never tried to change her, and he encouraged her appetite for new experiences—food, outings, sex.

She gazed down at the man she loved and leaned away. With a coy smile, she crossed her wrists behind her.

Vashien didn't take her bait. He kicked the door closed and stepped into the gutted two-story townhouse. "How many times did you fuck with my wings?"

Sparrow snorted and slouched before helping him undo the first two buttons of his shirt. "You can't count all of them. The first five were flirting," Sparrow argued quietly.

Vashien outstretched his wings, and she hugged him closer. They were gorgeous, easily her favorite part of him. She reached past his muscled shoulder and ran the back of the articulated claw of her ring along her favorite spot.

He crushed her against him, and Sparrow froze with excited anticipation. His breath tickled her neck as he grated, "You're going to get it."

"But *wheeeen* are you going to give it to me?" she breathed, wiggling her ass.

Sparrow's hair cascaded forward as Vashien leapt. With a single beat of his wings, they landed on the expansive loft on the second floor. She shrieked as he tossed her backward.

A brilliant light engulfed her as she instinctively changed into her cat form. She twisted in the air, getting her feet under her to land in the middle of their over-sized Artithian bed. Shifting back into a woman, Sparrow seductively crawled over the sky-blue sheets.

"Seventeen," Vashien answered, unbuttoning his shirt.

Seventeen, Sparrow mouthed as she brushed her fingertips over the black leather lingerie collar he'd chosen for her. Intent and will activated them. A flicker of power, embedded with her aching want for him, charged the magic spelled within it. Sparrow looked down at herself. Her dress was replaced with constricting leather. A buckled halter corset cinched her waist, accentuating the flare of her hips. Tall, belted boots covered the length of her legs.

She exposed her back to him and lowered her shoulders to the bed. The position lifted her ass, giving him the view her crotchless leather panties offered. She ached and needed him to fuck her.

Sparrow stretched her arms in front of her and turned to peer at him over her shoulder. "Why don't you spank me seventeen times and we'll call it even."

He undid his belt, pulling it free. The sound made Sparrow's toes curl. Her heart beat faster. The leather tip brushed the back of her thigh, and she closed her eyes, waiting for the stinging snap.

It skimmed over her ass and she dug her nails into the sheets, anticipating the slap of leather.

Vash pulled away without spanking her. Disappointed, Sparrow flopped over on to her side and rolled on to her back. He couldn't really be upset with her. They played this game every time he took her to Necromia.

Anytime he took her anywhere, really.

Staring at him upside down, she watched Vashien unbutton his shirt and gesture to the closet at the far end of his loft. "Get your harness, Sunshine. Orgasms will be your punishment tonight."

Sparrow snorted, rolling over and swinging her heels off the bed. "Sounds like a bribe," she said in a sing-song voice, waving her hand at him. "I could trace little circles on that spot you like while I ride you."

The mattress sank beside her, and Vashien's hand caged her throat. She pitched her head back to look up at him as his thumb dragged across her lips. He grinned when she opened them for him.

"Does my best girl want to be a princess or a slut tonight?" he asked, pressing his thumb past her lips.

Sparrow sucked obediently, closing her eyes as Vashien pulled her head back further. *I'm your slut. Punish me, Wing Daddy.*

He kissed her forehead tenderly as his hand came down hard on her ass. Sparrow whimpered, and Vashien spanked her again. Heat radiated across her bottom, and she arched her back in anticipation for more.

Vashien squeezed her tender flesh and whispered, "I'm going to add to your count every time you disobey me. You're at eighteen. Put on your harness before I make it nineteen."

Vashien leaned back, letting Sparrow up. She'd fight him until she deemed his patience earned her submission. He'd been a complete gentleman throughout dinner while she stroked his wings—making him hard. Behind closed doors, his princess became his slut.

Sparrow rolled over, laying her head on his lap. She walked her fingers to his waist and said, "You know… we could skip all this, and you could just fuck me. I know you've imagined everything you want to do to me."

She gazed up at him seductively, her bright green eyes veiled by her curled lashes. Her makeup was painstakingly applied to perfection. He wanted to ruin it while he fucked her mouth. "Oh, I'm going to do so many things to you, Sunshine," he said, gently brushing a blonde curl from her face. Her eyes gleamed and he smiled wickedly. "Nineteen."

"Are you serious?"

"Twenty."

"Stop, I'm going," she said in a rush.

Sparrow skipped to the closet she commandeered earlier on in their relationship, and Vash went to his nightstand. He pulled open the top drawer and removed Sparrow's favorite toys. Two small red lotus blossoms. Artithians lacked the ability to purr, and the flowers simulated the suction and vibrations vampires and shifters were capable of. Some men envied these other races, but Vashien never found himself among them. A purring mouth was too easy to simulate. Wings, on the other hand, were impossible to recreate. He pitied the ground-born. Couldn't imagine a life without feeling the soaring rush of an open sky.

"I don't see how you think this is a punishment," Sparrow grumbled as she clipped her newest satin harness in place.

He would enlighten her soon enough. "You won't need this," Vashien said, reaching behind her to unclasp her lingerie collar.

The strapped leather vanished, and he admired her generous curves wrapped like a gift. Harnesses could be made of any material, and this one looked more like lingerie. Wide ribbons of black satin circled her waist, connecting to more loops wrapped around each thigh. A length of satin ran along her spine, beginning at her garter belt and looping her throat.

Three ribbons hung from it. Two in the center, lining her back, and the other swung from her belt like a tail. The strips of satin could be spelled to repeat movements or be manipulated by his will.

Vashien's dark misted shard churned as he controlled the length of the fabric. They encircled Sparrow's breasts, squeezing and pinching her nipples. She moaned as he tugged harder.

"Pick what you want to be fucked with," Vash said, pulling his drawer open further.

She sat on the bed in front of him and unbuttoned his pants. "Can I pick you?" she asked breathlessly.

Vashien let her pull his cock free, hissing a breath as her lips closed over the head. She moaned, sending vibrations up his shaft as she leaned forward and took him deeper. He fisted her golden curls and thrust forward, pressing into her throat.

He groaned, leaning his head back as he fucked her mouth. His fingertips traced her jaw, brushing lower to her neck. "Oh, my best girl likes being my little slut? Have you missed having my cock in your mouth?"

His ray of sunshine clawed at his waist, taking his entire length. He held her there and brushed her cheek. "Eyes up."

She obeyed, and, Darkness, it made him hard. Her bright green eyes reminded him of the forest along the cliffs he once called home. As much as he loved how her eyes gleamed when he surprised her with jewelry, he equally loved seeing her makeup askew from tears with her mouth around his cock.

Vashien pulled back, and she whined. His breath caught as she leaned forward, taking him deep before sitting back on her heels.

Artithian curses spilled from his lips when she licked the tip of his cock.

"Please fuck me, Wing Daddy. I need your cock in my pussy," Sparrow pleaded before working him back into her throat.

"Not yet, Sunshine. Now pick the toy you want to be fucked with, or I'll choose for you," Vash groaned.

Sparrow reluctantly released him and yanked the teasing ribbons away from her breasts.

"Now, now," Vash said as the satin looped her wrists. He carefully drew them behind her. Using his will, he crossed the material behind her back to secure her and dragged the smooth fabric across her sides before following the curve of her breasts. One ribbon folded to pinch her nipple, and the other collected the small red lotus flower.

It glowed, pulsing in time with a low hum as its pedals began to sway. Sparrow's eyes widened, suddenly sorry for the way she acted tonight, he assumed. She made her bed, and he intended to fuck her in it.

"We'll start with three." Vash lowered the flower between her legs. He controlled it with his will and could sense the suction on her clit, controlling the vibrations, and even move the pedals.

Sparrow fell backward, pulling her legs together. "Darkness, Vash!" she cried, yanking against her bonds.

"Keep your legs spread, or I won't count these as part of your punishment," Vash said calmly. Sparrow panted, letting her legs fall wide as she tensed. He let her squirm, looking over his little Familiar's collection. She had toys varying in different lengths and thicknesses. Their colors ranged from realistic to more extravagant, like her newest sparkling, rose gold addition.

He recognized her shuttering breath, the way she trembled as she cried his name. He palmed her thigh. Fates, she was wet. He knelt and pulled her to him. "That's my best girl. Come for me," Vash said before greedily licking her desire.

She tremored against his tongue, squeezing him when he licked inside her. "Count them," he commanded.

"One." Sparrow's voice was sharp and shrill as she rode her pleasure.

"Good girl," Vash growled against her silken flesh. The ribbon lifted the blossom away, and Sparrow went boneless, catching her breath. He licked and kissed her clit, savoring the taste of her.

If she had paid attention, she would have noticed the flower glowed brighter, mirroring the intensity of its vibrations. He would increase them each time she came, then fuck her needy pussy.

He reached blindly into the drawer and feasted on her, grabbing her nearest toy. "Looks like we're breaking in your newest friend," Vashien teased. He kissed her inner thigh and asked, "Do you remember your safe word?"

Sparrow nodded vigorously. "Yes," she breathed, rolling her hips.

"Say it, so I know you remember," Vash said, sliding her rose gold cock through her folds.

She bucked her hips when he pressed the head to her opening. "Ground, the safe word is ground! Don't stop. Vash, please."

"That's my best girl," he said as he made use of his remaining ribbons.

One picked up the second lotus, and the other wrapped around the base of the cock he held. Vashien set the flowers on Sparrow's nipples, and she tensed, whimpering. Darkness, he loved the sounds she made. He spelled the third ribbon to fuck her slow and easy while he tongued her clit.

"Two," she said between panting breaths. Vashien lifted his head and moved a lotus to her clit. She screamed his name but kept her legs spread as he asked. "Three… three," she stammered.

Vashien worked her mercilessly as he stripped off his clothing. Sparrow was flushed and sweat slick by the time she reached ten. He leaned over her and loosened the loops restraining her arms. She reached for him immediately and he kissed her gently. When he lifted his head, her brows pinched. She moaned, writhing beneath him while the harness worked the rose gold cock in and out of her cunt.

"Roll over. I want you to lift your hips but keep your shoulders on the bed," Vash said at her lips. Sparrow rushed to obey him. He slapped her ass, eliciting a sweet cry from her lips.

"You know better than to close your legs. That's my best girl. Let me see how wet you are." Vash's hand slid up her back, and he gripped her waist, fucking her harder with the harness.

"Eleven," Sparrow cried breathlessly.

She spread her legs further, lowering her hips to her heels. Vashien's palm met her ass in a hard slap, and she bunched his sky-blue sheets in her hands "I said to lift your ass," Vash said gently, raising her hips to their original position. He leaned over her, wrapping his hand around her throat. She whimpered when he nipped her earlobe. "If you make me repeat myself. I'm going to fuck your ass."

Sparrow's slim shoulders tensed as her breathing turned ragged.

"Is that twelve, Sunshine?" Vashien asked, cupping her breast. He circled her nipple with the pad of his thumb, kissing the back of her neck. She nodded shakily and he pinched her tight peak, rolling it between his thumb and forefinger. "Say it, or it doesn't count."

"Twelve," she answered weakly.

Vashien licked and teased Sparrow as she took her punishment. He rasped, "My best girl is such a good slut for me," while he orchestrated her harness to drive her to her next orgasm. When she muttered, "Eighteen," he rolled her onto her back. At nineteen, the satin ribbon withdrew the rose gold cock.

Sparrow's forest green eyes were passion glazed; her makeup ruined. Ringlets of her blonde curls clung to her forehead and neck as she slowly blinked up at him.

Vashien hooked his arm under her leg and dragged her closer. He held her leg to his chest, lifting her ass off the bed. "You owe me one more," he growled.

She screamed his name as he thrusted into her wet cunt. He groaned, willing the little flowers to suck harder. He wanted to feel her coming on his cock. Her back bowed and Vash fucked her harder. He was much larger than her toys and stretched her to accommodate his size.

"You're such a good slut, taking all of my cock like this. Be my best girl and open your mouth," Vash groaned between his thrusts.

The satin ribbon brought her toy to her lips and Sparrow opened eagerly. "Such a good fucking girl," Vash grated. He used her harness to work her mouth, timing the deep thrusts with his own between her legs.

Moisture had collected on her lashes when Vash felt the first flutters around his cock. She squeezed him intimately, rolling her hips.

Twenty, she cried in his mind.

Vashien vanished the harness and her toys, lifting her into his arms. His wings encircled her, holding her close. She leaned against him, limp and completely spent. Her lips brushed the side of his neck as small sounds escaped her. He palmed her ass, holding her in place while he lost himself in her.

His arms tightened around her as his eyes squeezed shut. His wings snapped open, flaring behind him as he came. He cradled her against him, emptying himself deep inside her.

"You're such a good girl," Vash whispered, brushing his lips over her temple. "My best girl," he continued before wrapping his wings around her. "My Sunshine."

She moaned softly in agreement, resting against him. His chest ached at how she trusted him to take care of her. The first thing he needed to do was clean her up and bring her some water.

"I'll draw you a bath—"

"With bubbles," Sparrow interrupted him.

He smiled warmly, cradling her in his arms as he got to his feet. "With bubbles, and after you drink your water, I'll cook something for you."

"I don't want water. It's boring," Sparrow grumbled, leaning into his chest.

Of course it was, Vashien thought, gazing down at the Familiar who'd stolen his heart and become his home. Vashien stepped off the landing and spread his wings to land softly on the first floor.

Ice Cream and Waffles

Takes place after A Trial of Lace and Bone.

Vashien collected a perfectly smooth oval of vanilla cream with a turn of his wrist. He tipped it onto Sparrow's breakfast, carefully preserving its shape.

The busy night at Lost and Found had left him restless. He slipped away, donning a pair of loose-fitting trousers, and leaving Sparrow to doze in the loft while he cooked. His sunshine grew more irritable each day. The minor cut on the top of her thigh didn't mend within a few hours. Accelerated healing was the safest marker of eternal life. At twenty-seven, Sparrow's fears were valid, and he became acutely aware of what he'd taken for granted centuries ago.

His immortality was never a question. The strong, leathery wings against his back proclaimed he would be among the undying.

But Sparrow…

Vash lifted his gaze. The rustling of sheets and Sparrow's unhappy groan sounded from the loft that served as their bedroom. She would shower before waiting on the ledge for him. Artithians had little use for stairs when they could easily fly, but his little Familiar was wingless. He'd meant to have steps installed for her, but they'd spent so little time here it had slipped his mind.

This was the second Hunter's Moon they'd spent away from court. He thanked the Darkness Faye asked for space; vampires weren't exactly discreet under the blood-red moon. Vashien took a deep breath and thinned his lips as he stared out his living room windows. The dawning light crested over the mountains, signaling the end of the vampire's sacred night. Vash wouldn't return to court until late in the evening. He had absolutely no desire to stumble across Faye in a compromising position with the Shadow Prince—or worse, Voshki.

Vashien banished the unpleasant thoughts and focused on his task. He arranged curls of white chocolate shavings with plating tweezers. This presentation was hardly necessary, but the golden-brown waffle drizzled with freshly made blackberry compote would keep Sparrow's mind from fixating on her lack of immortality.

"If I jump, will you catch me?" Sparrow asked playfully.

Vashien wiped the perimeter of the plate and glanced up. She stood at the edge of the loft, leaning forward precariously to peer at the fifteen-foot drop. She pulled her wet golden ringlets to one side, but it was the bright red chemise that commanded his attention. The black lace-trimmed silk hugged the curve of her breasts and the outline of her nipples pressed against the thin fabric.

He stepped around the kitchen island, and Sparrow turned, placing her heels on the edge of the loft. She blinked at him over her shoulder as a mischievous, toothy grin spread over her lips.

"Sparrow—"

His warning was cut short as she dramatically brought the back of her hand to her forehead and leaned away, falling into the open air.

Vashien's heart thundered as he surged forward. He was airborne with the first beat of his wings and caught her on the second.

"Is this how we're starting our day?" he asked, landing softly on the first floor.

Sparrow snorted and traced her fingertips along his jaw. "You always catch me," she purred before wiggling out of his hold. "You made breakfast?"

Vashien's lashes lowered as she sauntered away. The slip she wore barely covered her perfectly shaped ass, and he was willing to bet she wasn't wearing anything under it. His cock hardened as he shifted his wings, following her.

Sparrow pressed her palm to the counter and vaulted up. The hem of her lingerie lifted as she twisted to sit on the counter, confirming Vash's suspicions. She pulled the silk over her hip on one side and frowned at the small injury.

"Can you redo the cut on my hip?" she asked.

Vashien stepped in front of her and smoothed his hand up her thigh. He called in his dagger, a companion to his Artithian war blade. He nicked her and Sparrow winced, looking away as tiny drops of blood rose along the incision.

"What if my immortality never takes?" she asked quietly.

He hated the defeat in her voice. Her self-assured confidence was the thing he loved most about her. She woke each morning and checked to see if the cut had healed completely over the course of the night.

The wound persisted, stealing the fire of her soul.

"You're only twenty-seven. I'm sure it will seat any day now," Vash reassured her as he vanished his blade. She swallowed thickly and didn't answer. He leaned into her and pulled her close, dragging her ass to the edge of the counter. His lips brushed her forehead, and she softened in his arms. If food wasn't enough of a distraction, he would use her temper against her.

Vash glided his thumb across her lower back and teasingly whispered, "You'll be immortal because you're too much trouble. The Darkness doesn't want you back."

"I am a *joy* to be around," she corrected.

Her hands smoothed over his shoulders as she pressed her lips and glared up at him. Her temper ignited the fire living in her eyes. Vash grinned and leaned down, putting his wings in easy reach.

"Never a dull moment, sunshine," Vashien rasped.

The tip of her finger stroked the inside of his wing, where the membrane met his back. Pleasure shot through him, and he exhaled a shuddering breath.

"You're lucky to have me," she breathed, tracing circles near the heavy bones anchoring his wing. She slipped her other hand into his trousers and his breath caught when she fisted his cock. Her fingers gripped him, stroking up and down while she expertly twisted her wrist.

Pleasure overtook Vashien's mind. He held her tighter, rocking his hips to fuck her hand. "Are you trying to get me to come in my pants?"

"I'm trying to get you to fuck me," she laughed.

Vash grinned and gently pulled her hands away before straightening. He brought the small bowl of blackberry compote closer and dipped a finger in it. Sparrow's green eyes gleamed as she stared up at him. He painted her mouth with the dark puree, and she licked her lips.

His gaze never left her pout as he said, "Good girls get fucked, sunshine."

"I'll be a good girl," Sparrow answered on the heels of his statement. She took his wrist and sensually licked the blackberry sauce off the tip of his finger.

"My best girl?" Vashien asked, adding another. She sucked as he pressed deeper, slowly fucking her mouth.

Sparrow moaned and let the straps of her chemise slip off her shoulders. The silk fell lower, exposing her full breasts.

"Pinch your nipples for me," he grated. She leaned back and Vashien followed her, undoing his pants. Sparrow squeezed her breasts and rolled the tight peaks between her thumb and forefinger.

Vashien withdrew from her mouth and captured her throat. He applied pressure on either side of her neck and pushed up her skirt before grinning. "Harder, sunshine. Take your punishment."

Sparrow panted beneath him, pinching and twisting her hard peaks. Vashien angled his wings forward and hooked the bend of her knees. He leaned closer, pinning her legs on either side of her shoulders. She was spread wide and wet.

Gorgeous and his.

Vashien's lashes lifted and found her watching him. He held her stare as he pressed forward, stretching her to take his cock. She moaned and he thrusted into her roughly, forcing her to take him. Sparrow's eyes fluttered closed as she strained against his wings to close her legs.

"Eyes on me, sunshine," he teased, driving several more inches into her. She looked up at him and he rewarded her obedience with slow strokes until she'd taken his entire length.

"Play with your clit," Vashien said, gripping her hips. "Faster.

The way you like it. That's my best girl," he groaned, fucking her harder. She squeezed his cock intimately and Vash leaned so close her nipples dragged across his chest with each thrust.

He kissed her softly and whispered against her lips. "If you come without my permission, I'm going to tie your hands behind your back and spell a harness to fuck your ass. It'll be rough, and you'll take your punishment until you make me come. I'll let you decide if you want to use your pussy or your mouth."

"What?" Sparrow gasped, blinking as her lips parted.

Vash eased the pressure on her throat but kept her caged under his grasp. "Orgasms are for good girls, sunshine."

"Vash, please, I'm going to come," she begged.

"Do it and I'll tie you to this counter with your legs spread," he warned. "Do you want your nipples and clit teased while a spelled harness fucks all of your holes?"

Sparrow squeezed her eyes shut, panting as a flush crept down her throat to her breasts. Vashien straightened his index finger and angled her head toward him. "Look at me when I'm fucking you."

She whimpered but opened her eyes. His feast spread beneath him, watching him helplessly as his cock worked in and out of her slick cunt.

"Wing Daddy, please let me come. I'll be good. I'll play nice. I'll do whatever you want," Sparrow whined and begged between breathless pants.

Vashien smiled and edged her until she shamelessly rolled her hips. Until tears tracked from the corners of her eyes, and she trembled uncontrollably.

Until she could no longer form the words to beg for her release.

"Vashien, please," she cried sometime later.

He pressed the heel of his palm above the junction of her thighs and groaned, "Come for me, sunshine. I want to feel your pussy squeezing my cock." Her inner walls clenched around him, and he took her harder. "That's my best girl."

Vashien tilted his head up, concentrating on the feel of her and the moans slipping past her lips. He drove into her harder, his hand closing on either side of her throat. Tension filled him, but he needed more.

He released her legs and pulled her into his arms while keeping his desperate rhythm. "Touch my wings," he rasped against her curls.

"Come for me, Wing Daddy. I need you. Please," she said in a breathless whisper as her fingertips stroked the inside of his wing.

Vashien's breath locked in his throat as he thrusted into her a final time. His legs shook as his balls tightened. "Darkness," he cursed as he emptied himself inside her. His chest heaved as he fought to catch his breath. His knees nearly buckled when Sparrow idly stroked his wing again. "You can stop now."

Sparrow tightened her thighs over his waist. "No."

"You're asking for it, sunshine."

She rolled her hips and traced curling lines along his wing. Pleasure lashed through him and Vashien's brow pinched as he groaned.

"Are you going to give it to me?" she asked coyly.

"Maybe after breakfast," he said, untangling himself from her embrace.

Sparrow pulled off the chemise bunched around her middle. "I'll need to get this laundered to get the blood out of it," she said, inspecting the silk.

Vashien dragged her plate of waffles closer and furrowed his brow when she leaned away from him. "I'll buy you another one if it got ruined."

"No. I just… give me this," she said, snatching the nearest kitchen towel. She pressed her thumb into her thigh and scoured the light smear of blood. She swiped over it once. Then again as her breathing slowed and her eyes widened.

Vashien's chest constricted as he chuckled, gingerly running the pad of his thumb over the clean unbroken skin at the top of Sparrow's thigh. An eternity stretched before her, and he would spend the rest of his days by her side.

"I'm immortal…" Sparrow whispered, staring at her hip. She lifted her head and gave him a toothy grin. "You get this pussy forever."

The excitement in her eyes dulled and the corners of her mouth fell the next instant, slicing cleanly into Vashien's heart.

"Cut me again," she said, void of emotion.

Vashien cupped her cheek. "You don't need to do it again, sunshine. You're immortal."

Sparrow snorted. "What if I just healed myself while you had me dick-notized?" He laughed, and she swatted his chest hard enough to leave a red mark. "Stop laughing and do it. I need to be sure," she said in a quieter voice.

Vashien called in his dagger and Sparrow tensed, turning away. He made the same small cut on the top of her thigh and kissed her temple. "It'll heal up in a couple of hours."

Sparrow inspected the beads of blood rising along the thin line. "This is going to be the longest three hours of my life."

"I'll take you to a bookstore if you promise not to knock over any tables." Vashien grinned when she glared up at him.

"Orrrrrr I could watch you cook…" Sparrow said, tugging on his belt loops. "Naked."

Vashien leaned into her and met her lips in a gentle kiss. "I'm sure that can be arranged."

A CAT IN THE KITCHEN

Takes place after A Trial of Lace and Bone.

The soft hiss of a spray and clean cotton over wood grain soothed Vashien. He wiped down the last bar and inhaled deeply, smiling at the understated scent of pine. It was part of the ambiance he'd spelled into his eatery. One of the many things he curated into Lost and Found's interior to reflect Artithian customs. Vashien folded the bar towel and grinned. *Well, not the white marble and gold inlays the royals were obsessed with.* Vashien wasn't noble and grew up on the mountain cliffsides of his home realm. The open beams, scent of pine, and rustic charm he'd created in this space let him feel closer to his family when he was away.

Vashien paused at the clink of metal on glass. The last of his staff had left more than thirty minutes ago. When it sounded again, he followed it, heading toward the kitchen.

Dark gray light flickered over him as he shielded himself. The cold familiarity of his war blade rested in his grip. Vashien pushed his senses past his physical body and let his shields drop when he met Sparrow's awareness. He vanished his weapon and crossed into the kitchen, making a metal note to teach her to properly shield her mind. The defensive precaution wouldn't stop anyone from feeling a presence, but it would conceal the distinct feel of her.

Sparrow was seated on his stainless-steel counter with her short ox-blood skirt hiked up around her hips—blissfully unaware he'd have to sanitize the surface, again. While he didn't mind her perfectly rounded ass on his prep table, his paying customers would be less obliging to say the least.

Vashien came to a stop as he assessed the rest of the counter. His sunshine had taken it upon herself to sample his dessert menu and was surrounded by half a dozen small plates of varied cakes and sweets.

"What are you doing?" he asked.

Sparrow licked chocolate syrup off her thumb suggestively and smiled up at him. "Waiting for you."

"Who let you in?" And how hadn't he noticed her for the last half hour.

"I'm the boss's girl," Sparrow said with a wave of her hand. "They always let me in. How'd you think I got into your office all the time?" She leaned forward and hooked her fingers between the buttons of his shirt, pulling him closer. "We haven't fucked in the kitchen yet," Sparrow purred.

Vashien assessed the plates as she exposed his chest. "Did you have to take one bite out of all of them?"

Sparrow gripped his belt and tilted her head back. Mischief always permeated her bright green eyes when she reached for an innocent expression. "I forgot which one was my favorite."

"And you're going to eat these?" Vashien said, pointing at the myriad of dishes.

"Faye will help me, and Kimber will probably steal half of them. Unless…" Sparrow leaned back on her hands. The strap of her slinky black top slipped down her shoulders. Vashien's gaze lowered to the thin material scarcely covering Sparrow's divine breasts. She swept her finger though raspberry mousse and traced the curve of her breast. "Did you want to have dessert with me, Wing Daddy?"

Sparrow closed her eyes as Vashien leaned closer. His short dark hair fell forward, brushing her collarbone, and a breath slipped from her at the first feel of his lips. She gripped the base of his wing as he seared her with a hot sweep of his tongue. Darkness, she needed his cock inside her. Thrusting into her until her eyes fluttered closed and she couldn't think.

He raised his head and Sparrow leaned up expecting a kiss. He drew back with a smirk but kept their distance intimate.

"Good girls get fucked, sunshine. Bad girls get punished," he said, running the bend of his finger along her neckline.

He circled her nipples with each pass and Sparrow breathlessly whined, "I've been mostly good." He didn't really want her to be good and Sparrow had too much fun playing with him. She enjoyed dancing at the edge of her boundaries, but the real thrill was antici-pating what he would do with her. These punishments were more of a game than a discipline. The moment she objected he would stop.

The only problem was she never wanted him to.

Vashien took the bottom edge of her shirt in both of his hands and Sparrow jumped as he ripped the material in two.

"Hey, I might be immortal now but don't damage the merchan-dise," Sparrow said, staring at the tattered remains of her shirt.

"I am extremely careful with you," Vashien rasped. He smoothed his hand up her thigh and narrowed his eyes as his hand slid smoothly to the top of her hip. "You're not wearing anything under this."

"Don't look so disappointed," she purred, wrapping her legs around his waist. "I was hoping to get laid, so I saved you the trouble."

"Did you now?" Vashien asked before nipping her bottom lip.

Sparrow moaned in agreement and pulled open his belt. "I missed you," she breathed. She'd needed to feel him since she woke up this morning alone in their bed.

Vashien captured her wrists in one hand. "And instead of wait-ing for me, you decided to take one of each dessert and contaminate my counters."

She looked at the elegant plates on either side of her and shrugged. "I mean… If you already have to sanitize the kitchen we may as well, get dirty."

He arched a brow at her, and Sparrow tightened her legs around

Vashien's waist, pulling him closer. His lying face might say he didn't approve of her being in his kitchen, but his hardening cock said otherwise. Sparrow wondered if he'd want her throat before he fucked her or if he would tell her to clean him after he came in her pussy.

Sparrow exhaled a soft breath at the memory. The taste of them on her lips as she got on her knees and sucked his still hard cock clean.

"I think I will share a dessert with you."

Vashien's voice drew her back to the present. He released her wrists and his palm pressed into the front of her neck. Heat pooled between her legs as he guided her down. The chill of the metal countertop bit through the thin material still covering her back and her nipples hardened into tight peaks.

Glass slid over steel and Sparrow turned her head to see Vashien pulling the raspberry mousse closer. He dragged the back of the spoon through it, carefully coating the metal.

"Spread your legs, sunshine. Wider," he rasped, lowering his gaze. "That's my best girl. Now finger yourself."

A smile crept over Sparrow's lips. She reached between her thighs and ran a finger across her spread pussy, from her opening to her clit. Pleasure ricocheted through her as she circled her clit once. Twice.

Vashien palmed her breast roughly before slapping her soft flesh. It amplified the stinging pleasure when he pinched her nipple. Sparrow gasped as he tugged while heat spread over the side of her breast.

"I said finger yourself, sunshine."

Sparrow lowered her touch and pressed a fingertip inside as she met his hazel eyes. She didn't want to finger herself and a punishing fuck while he held her down was exactly what she needed.

"If you don't stretch that pretty pussy around your fingers, I'll phase us home and make you finger your ass instead," Vashien said, leaning closer. "Or is that what you want, sunshine. Bent over with your shoulders on the bed? If I have take you home, I'll use a vibrator on your pretty clit while you fuck your ass. You're going to edge yourself for an hour and if you come..."

Vashien's eyes darkened as he grinned. Waiting.

"You start my time again," Sparrow answered as she thrusted

a finger into her slick heat. Being edged for an hour wasn't how she wanted to spend the rest of her evening. "Please fuck me, Wing Daddy."

The callused skin over the bones of his wings scraped over her thighs as he forced her legs apart. "That would have worked if you didn't make a mess of my kitchen."

"I need you," Sparrow breathed.

Vashien glanced down at her spread pussy, at her finger obediently thrusting in and out of her. "Fuck your pretty pussy, sunshine. We both know that's not how you like it."

Sparrow panted adding a second finger.

"Use three. That's my best girl. Show me how much you want my cock."

She worked in a third and was rewarded with a careful tightening grip on either side of her neck. Fucking herself while he watched made her wet but wasn't enough to make her come. She rolled her hips, imagining it was Vash's fingers working in and out of her, stretching her to take him deep. Her breath became ragged, and she reached between her legs. She pressed hard, circling her clit.

Cold shocked her nipple and Sparrow gasped. Vashien bent over her the next moment, his tongue hot as he licked the chill away.

Sparrow's fingers slowed as she turned her head, unable to see with the way Vash held her neck. "What is that?" Sparrow breathed.

"I'm having dessert," Vashien said holding a spoon in her view. The back of it was coated in a mauve cream. Sparrow narrowed her eyes, but her curiosity evaporated when the pressure on her throat increased a fraction. "And if you stop fucking yourself again… I'll take you home, sunshine—and we'll do this proper."

Sparrow nodded and sucked a breath when cold slid over the tight peak of her breast. She moaned as he squeezed her soft flesh and sucked until her nipple warmed. He watched her fingers work, his voice taking a rough edge as he spoke to her while he licked away the cream he meticulously painted her nipples with.

"We both know you like to be fucked harder than that."

"Deeper, sunshine."

"That's my best girl."

Her pleasure intensified as her head swam and Vashien eased his hold. He repeated her ecstasy, watching her as he regarded her flushed expression with a reverent longing.

"Fuck me, Vash. Please," Sparrow moaned. She needed more than her fingers could give and Vash's teasing mouth only intensified the ache she couldn't fill.

Vashien gently tugged her nipple and grinned. "Does your greedy cunt need my cock?"

Sparrow nodded. The heavy bones of his wings dug into her thighs as she strained against him. Fucking Artithians and their wings. It wasn't fair he had extra appendages to hold her down.

"I'll have you screaming my name as soon as I finish my dessert," he said, painting her nipple with his torturously cold sweet.

Sparrow wasn't sure how much time passed. Vashien savored each lick while simultaneously giving her no quarter. Anytime her movements slowed, he rasped, "Fuck your pussy the way I would, or I'll take you home and call in late tomorrow."

She was sweat slick and breathless when the soft click of metal on glass sounded beside her. Vashien released her throat and smoothed his hand down her body as he undid his belt. He yanked it free and set it beside her on the counter. Sparrow turned toward it, continuing her frantic rhythm obediently. She might have asked him to bend her over and spank her ass with it as he fucked her. But that would delay her reward and she needed to feel his cock buried inside her.

Vashien undid his pants and pulled his cock free. His lashes lowered as he watched her fuck her spread pussy. Sparrow moaned when he fisted his cock and stroked. Once. Twice.

"Show me the mess you made," Vashien growled.

Sparrow hesitated for a moment, lost in the feel of her giving flesh and his head against her fingers. She raised her hand between them, the proof of her desire coating her touch. He leaned back, nudging the tip of his cock into her cunt before moving his thumb lower. Sparrow's eyes fluttered closed when he teased the entrance of her ass.

Vashien took a measured stroke, stretching her wider than her fingers ever could. She moaned, rolling her hips—needing more than the teasing inches he'd given her.

"You're going to finger your ass while I fuck you, sunshine."

Sparrow didn't hesitate, lifting her hips and sliding her hand beneath her. Darkness, she had made a mess. Her arousal coated her ass and dripped to the counter. She stared up at him and pressed a finger into her ass as a flush crept over her cheeks. A heat rooted in anticipation instead of embarrassment or nerves. He loved and respected her, feeding every appetite she possessed. He never judged her or looked at her differently and this freedom chained her to him.

She smiled, realizing they now had an eternity before them.

Vashien gripped her hips and drove into her with punishing thrusts. He swept his green membranous wings back, stretching them behind him. Sparrow wrapped her legs around his lean waist and stared at the lights overhead illuminating his wings. Pinks and browns backlit against the dark green and outlined the pattern of his veins. She wanted to touch them. Stroke the sensitive spot where they connected to his back.

"Add a second. I want to feel you fucking your ass," he growled.

Sparrow tensed as her pleasure mounted. She pressed a second finger to her entrance but couldn't work it in. "I can't. It's too tight."

Vashien dragged her against him without missing a stroke. Her arms circled his neck and Sparrow's head fell back. He thrust into her harder and his seeking fingers found her ass. "Take it and come for me," he rasped.

Sparrow cried out as he forced two fingers into her ass. "Vash," she breathed. She'd never felt so filled. So completed and possessed.

His fingers drove into her with each thrust. The tension building within her turned into the sweetest agony and Vashien groaned, "Come for me, sunshine."

She gripped the heavy bones anchoring his wings as the tension snapped. She screamed his name and came hard, shaking in his arms.

"That's my filthy girl," he said, showing her no mercy as he fucked her harder.

Vashien claimed her mouth in a kiss, forcing her jaw wide as he invaded every part of her. She clung to him as wave after wave of blinding ecstasy crashed through her.

He withdrew his fingers and clutched her against him, driving into her a final time. His cock pulsed as he came, and Sparrow panted against his shoulder.

"If I knew you were going to fuck me like that, I would have done this a long time ago," Sparrow said, reaching down to stroke the inside of his wing.

He tensed around her and exhaled a sharp breath at her ear. "You're asking for it."

"But you're so fun to tease," Sparrow purred, snuggling closer to him.

"We should get you cleaned up. I'll run you a bath and get you some water before I come back to clean up," Vashien said, holding her against him as he stepped away from the counter. He lifted his chin at the myriad of plates and asked, "Did you want any of these?"

"Bring them with us. Kimber and Faye will want them when they wake up."

Vashien pulled away enough to give her a stern look. "I am *not* feeding your family sex desserts."

"They're fine. You're acting like you had your dick in them," Sparrow huffed.

He gestured at the mess she left on the counter and she snorted in response. "I'll bring your sisters a clean batch. Do you want any of these before I throw them out."

She narrowed her eyes and gave him a toothy grin. "But sex desserts are okay for me to eat."

"Darkness, what snack do you want for your bath woman?"

Sparrow rolled her hips, taking his semi-hard cock deeper and smiling when he groaned. "The chocolate one is my favorite," she said pointing at the cake he'd made for Faye's birthday a couple years ago.

Vashien took the plate and pressed a kiss to her temple before phasing them to Anaria.

Rune, Faye & Voshki

His Dark Queen

Takes place between chapter 63 and 64 of Invoking the Blood.

Voshki slowly unbuttoned his black dress shirt, contemplating all the ways he could make his queen beg before he allowed her to come. He and the Shadow Prince had an agreement where they spent an evening or two every few weeks in Faye's company. While they could never be truly alone, he looked forward to his uninterrupted nights.

Faye sat back on her heels at the center of their dark sheets, wearing the custom lingerie collar he'd selected for her. His cock hardened at the sight. The crimson leather suited her figure perfectly. The Shadow Prince would agree if he ever stopped lying to himself.

Voshki admired the satin-topped black stockings, held in place by a leather garter belt. He imagined beginning at her ankle and trailing teasing nips and kisses up his queen's stunning legs. But his dark eyes were drawn higher. The bra was the reason he acquired *this* collar in particular. The straps of supple leather looked more like a harness, outlining Faye's high breasts. He preferred his queen exposed and on display—and soon she would be breathless, pleading for his cock.

His queen crawled to the edge of their bed as he approached. Her lightning-streaked midnight gaze flicked over his chest, trailing lower as he shrugged out of his tailored shirt.

She settled to her knees, running her taupe-colored nails under the edge of the blood red collar as she glanced down at herself. "This doesn't cover much."

Voshki straightened the strip of leather. He ordered it specifically to lay flat against her collarbone, leaving the slender column of her neck bare for his fangs.

"You look beautiful," he said, leaning into her. The breathy sigh he adored slipped past her lips as he glided a single black tipped claw down the front of her throat. "Do you want to be tended to," Voshki asked as his touch slid past her shoulders, tracing the outline of her breast. He pinched her nipple, tugging lightly as Faye's nails dug into his waist. Her lips parted and Voshki added pressure until she moaned against his mouth.

"Or fucked," Voshki finished with a smirk.

"Fuck me," she breathed.

Voshki purred as her lips brushed over his. He nipped her, not satisfied with his queen's answer. "With what?"

"Please, Voshki," Faye whispered, palming his cock through his trousers.

He groaned, dragging her against him. The pulse point in her throat fluttered, making his fangs ache. "*Fuck me* could mean any number of things, vsenia. Do you want to lie back and spread your legs for me? Show me your pretty cunt while I fuck you with my will? Should I buy you a harness to keep a replica of my cock deep inside you? There are even ones spelled to fuck you. Would you like that? To be stretched and filled as I ravage your mouth."

A deep blush colored her cheeks and Voshki seized on the scent of her heightening arousal. He stifled the urge to pin her beneath him and sink his fangs into her throat. Drinking her as he took her with long, hard strokes.

"You like when I speak filth to you," Voshki purred in her ear. "Tell me how you want to be fucked, or I'll buy you a harness and use my imagination."

His queen gripped the front of his throat and ran the heel of her palm down his hardened length. "Fuck me, I want your cock between my legs."

Voshki tangled his hand in her hair and made a fist, angling her head up. "I want to feel your lips around my cock first. Be a good girl and show me how much you want it."

His hand slipped from her hair, and she eagerly reached for the closest pillow. He unfastened his pants, disrobing as she tossed the cushion at his feet. Faye lowered herself before him, calling to his vampiric instincts. She understood his craving for rough play. His need to possess her. How he worshipped her even as she knelt before him, submitting to his will.

She was the dark queen he waited his entire life for.

Voshki groaned as Faye stroked his shaft, taking the tip of his cock past her wine-colored lips. She rocked forward, sucking and licking while she held his gaze.

"Open your mouth wider. Take more of my cock," Voshki grated. She obeyed and he hissed a breath. "Yes, just like that. You're such a good girl."

Faye worked his considerable length, moaning as she took him deeper. Her kisses were too gentle, her strokes too light. He needed more, needed to fuck her mouth.

He gathered her hair and caressed her cheek. "How deep can you take me?"

Faye pulled him from her mouth and cupped his balls, continuing to slide her fist along his shaft. "Not as rough as last time," she said sternly.

Voshki smiled down at her. "Yes, my queen. Push on my waist if it's too much." Faye kissed the tip; the warmth of her mouth enveloped him as she flicked and teased him with her tongue. Voshki gnashed his teeth when he touched the back of her mouth. He wanted nothing more than to hold her still and drive his cock further.

Fucking her throat would take time and patience. Something the Shadow Prince should teach her as it encompassed most of his fantasies.

Voshki pulled back a fraction and tightened his grip on Faye's dark hair. "Here?"

She looked up at him through her dark lashes and nodded.

He held her in place and took a measured stroke, watching her reaction as he thrusted harder. She moaned and her hand shot to his waist. Voshki slowed but his queen dug her nails in, encouraging him to take her harder.

Darkness, she was fucking perfect.

"Good girl," Voshki groaned. "You're taking my cock so well. Are you aching?" Faye moaned, her answer sending vibrations through his shaft. "Should I fuck your pretty cunt?"

Please, Voshki, I need you, Faye cried through his mind.

"Do you?" he asked as his fangs sharpened with dark possession. "Finger yourself and show me how wet you are."

She blinked up at him and obeyed, reaching between her thighs. Her lids slid closed as she tensed, rocking on her hand. Voshki growled and her eyes snapped open. "You'll come on my cock, or I'll edge you until morning."

She stilled, whimpering around his length and he nearly spilled into her mouth. Voshki lifted her into his arms, guiding her legs around his lean waist. "Do you have something to show me, love?" he asked.

Her cheeks pinkened as she lifted her hand between them. Desire coated her index and middle finger.

"Just two?" Voshki teased. "Hardly a substitution for my cock, vsenia."

"Voshki, please," Faye begged.

He purred, moving them onto the bed. "Let me taste you." She turned her head to the side, exposing the slender column of her neck. His queen was so wet, desperate for his fangs and his cock.

She turned back to him as he lifted her hand. Voshki held her gaze, licking the arousal from her fingers before his lips closed over them. He sucked and Faye moaned, rolling her hips.

His mind hazed with the need to possess her. He pinned her waist against him and thrusted into her.

"Voshki!" Faye screamed.

He rose to his knees, holding her against him with one hand and steadied himself on the headboard with the other. She leaned back on his arm as he drove several more inches into her, taking her in a merciless rhythm.

She tensed, squeezing her thighs over his waist with bruising force. She panted and moaned, looking up at him as she pressed her fingers into his mouth, mimicking his thrusts.

Turnabout is fair play? he asked in her mind.

Her back bowed as she cried out. Voshki sucked and licked his queen's fingertips as she stroked into his mouth. The cries he elicited past her lips were a sweet melody he would never tire of.

Voshki thrusted into her, intoxicated by the scent, and feel of her. Faye's nails dug into his forearm as her fingers slipped from his mouth. She gripped the front of his throat, squeezing.

"Harder, don't stop," she cried.

Voshki obeyed her, leaning closer. "Does my queen want to come?"

Her breaths grew shorter as a flush spread over her breasts. Voshki purred, she was so close. He considered sitting back on his heels. There were few things he loved more than letting her writhe on his cock—desperate to come.

His queen begged so sweetly but would edge him as viciously as he edged her.

He grazed his fangs over her throat and a breathy cry slipped from her parted lips. It was tempting to drag out their game, but he would grant her a reprieve. His fangs sank deep. Her blood coated his tongue. Dark and rich. Electrifying his senses.

Faye trembled in his arms. "Voshki," she cried. Her inner walls fluttered around his cock, squeezing him intimately as she cried his name again and again.

His shoulders tensed as he fucked her harder, chasing his own pleasure as he clutched her against him and growled. Voshki thrusted into her a final time, cursing in High Tongue as he spent deep inside of her. Euphoria blanketed his mind as he held her close, drawing ragged breaths. He groaned as his cock twitched, pouring more of himself into her.

Faye hugged him close, tangling her hands in his hair. He turned toward her, nuzzling her dark tress. "I love you, vsenia."

"I love you too," she said.

Her words a breathless sigh.

Bound in Shadows

Takes place between chapter 84 and 85 of Invoking the Blood.

Faye secured Rune's forearms behind his back, looping the crimson silk into an intricate design. They sat at the end of their bed, surrounded by an assortment of candles she picked out for the evening. Her selection ranged from multi-wicked towers to glimmering tea lights. The flickers of hellfire scattered across their nightstands, and Rune's desk situated beneath two thin glass windows, bathed their room in a soft romantic glow.

Her vampire waited patiently as she finished his bindings. The task soothed and aroused her in equal portion, melting away her anxiety. In less than a week's time, she would stand before the High Council and Rune would be forced to answer Alister's request for her formal announcement. He was ready to sacrifice his social standing and announce himself as her whore. Faye would never allow it, and even though she'd found an executable loophole with Sadi's help… The details of their plan plagued her.

But not tonight, Faye thought as she finished the last silk knot. Tonight, her troubled mind would quiet as she found bliss with the two men she loved.

She leaned forward, resting her head on Rune's shoulder as she pulled the last section of red silk. She inhaled deeply, breathing in his scent of amber and sandalwood. Darkness, she wanted him. Each brush of skin, the feel of his chiseled body beneath her fingertips, tempted her from her work. She wanted to straddle his waist and sling her red tie over the back of his neck. Heat pooled between her thighs at the thought of his thick cock stretching her. She would take him into her body and use the silk for leverage as she rode him.

Faye bit the inside of her lip. The fantasy was tempting, but she had other desires whispering through her mind. She inspected her silken artwork before kissing the edge of Rune's shoulder. He purred as she palmed his cock and stroked him through his slacks. She leaned closer, pressing her breasts to his back.

"I'll have to tie you up more often if it gets you this hard," Faye breathed near his ear.

He turned toward her as the corner of his mouth lifted into a smirk. "I have been scenting your arousal for more than an hour, vsenia."

She reached lower, cupping him before running her nails from base to tip. "Are you hungry for a taste?"

"Famished," he answered, leaning back. Faye's breaths shallowed as her gaze dropped to his smooth, firm lips, and all the pleasure they promised. "How will you have me, my queen?" he murmured.

"On your knees," she whispered before touching her lips to his. A quick chaste kiss.

Phantom hands caressed her cheek and under her jaw, sliding into her hair. Rune held her with his magic, and he deepened the kiss. She opened for him, gliding her tongue against his as he languidly stroked into her mouth.

Faye nicked her lip on his canine. They were far more pronounced and sharper than usual. If he was this hard, his fangs would be aching. She grinned, pressing her tongue to the tip and was rewarded with his throaty groan. His phantom hands angled her head higher and he lightly sucked on her tongue.

She wrapped her arms around his neck, threading her fingers through his long white-blonde hair. Hands squeezed her breasts and Faye's eyes shot open as phantom mouths sucked and licked her nipples, mimicking Rune's kiss.

She moaned, torn between begging him to fuck her and recreating the first fantasy she entertained of him during her bath all those months ago. Darkness, she was so wet, aching like she'd been when they returned from the brothel. Faye flattened her hand over the hard plains of his chest, and he pulled back. His shadowed touch evaporated the moment he broke their kiss.

Faye called her riding crop and teasingly glided the flat leather tab over Rune's shoulder. She followed his throat, moving higher and stopping beneath his chin. He smiled and remained still. "You wish to have me beneath your crop?"

She flicked the square of leather away and kissed the corner of his mouth. "I wish to have you on your knees."

"As you command," Rune purred.

He stood and stepped between her legs, admiring the sheer gray negligee she'd chosen for the evening. It was classically tasteful, accented in white lace. The style Rune preferred her to wear in the bedroom. A stark contrast to the straps of leather and lingerie collars Voshki purchased for her.

She watched his muscles twist and flex as he kneeled before her. His pale blue eyes were clear of Voshki's shadows, but his stare was no less predatory. The sight of him on his knees with his hands bound behind his back thrilled her. Tension edged his every movement and Faye wondered how long Rune's obedience would last. How long she could play this game before he pinned her beneath him and ruthlessly fucked her. She arched her back pressing her nipples into the sheer material.

Phantom hands swiftly gripped her waist and dragged her roughly to the end of the bed. Faye flushed as more shadowed hands spread her legs. Rune's hair was cool against her inner thigh as he leaned closer. He stopped at the hem of her lingerie and Faye bit the inside of her lip.

She didn't expect the intoxicating way he remained in control even as he obeyed her every word. His mouth warmed her inner thigh and he moved higher, kissing her clit through the sheer fabric.

"Lift your skirt, love," Rune crooned. He sucked her clit beneath the thin material when she didn't immediately do as he asked. Faye's breath caught as his purr vibrated through her. Intensifying her pleasure.

The tension in her body coiled as she rolled her hips. Faye moaned, silently pleading for more. Rune drove her pleasure, taking her to the very edge and when the tension grew so taut, she was about to break—he stopped.

"Rune," she panted. A single touch would have her coming. She writhed beneath him, a moment from begging for mercy when amused pale blue eyes met hers.

"Would you like to lift your skirt now, vsenia?" he asked with a smirk.

Faye had initially hesitated because she wasn't wearing anything under her lacey slip, but her sweet vampire had a gift for sexually frustrating her past her nerves. She leaned back on one hand and crossed her legs behind him. She slowly pulled the hem of her skirt higher. His dark lashes lowered as he tracked her movements.

"And if I asked you to worship me for hours while you stroke yourself, would you do it," Faye asked.

Rune pinned her with his pale blue gaze and veined misted shadows crept from the corners of his eyes. "I am not the shy variable in our equation, vsenia. If you desire my tongue on your clit while I stroke my cock, you need only ask, love," he said playfully. He held her stare and licked through her slick folds, slow and deliberate, flicking his tongue where she was most sensitive.

Faye fell back against their dark sheets, dragging her heel over his bound arms and up his muscular back. She swatted his shoulder with her riding crop. "Harder."

Rune roughened his purr as his phantom hands lifted her ass off the bed, angling her hips like an offering. Faye panted her breaths as he pulled back and canted his head. A phantom mouth replaced his, sucking and purring on her clit.

"You are so beautiful," he whispered before moving lower to lick inside her.

"Deeper," Faye begged.

Rune obliged her, thrusting his tongue into her cunt. Pleasure radiated through her, intensifying her tension, but it wasn't enough to make her come. When she was breathless and covered in a thin layer of perspiration, she brushed the crop over his shoulder. Faye wet her lip as she exhaled. Rune's long white-blonde hair had fallen forward, sweeping over her hip with his movements. She traced the chiseled cuts of muscle over his side with her riding crop. She brought it higher, pushing his hair aside to watch him worshiping at her altar.

Her inner walls tightening over his tongue. His brow pinched and Faye moaned as he licked deeper. His mouth was open wide over her slit. A muscle in his jaw ticked rhythmically as he rocked forward in subtle motions, fucking her with his tongue.

He pulled back. His lips glistened in the candlelight with her desire. He caught her gaze. Strain and need tinged his stare. He blinked and sank his fangs into her inner thigh.

The feigned sensation of his cock thrusting into her had Faye screaming. It withdrew as he released his bite and returned as he drank.

"Rune—"

Her cries were strangled by pleasure, and she came hard. Her channel squeezed but his cock wasn't stretching her the way she desperately needed. The acute pleasure cascading through her body glittered through her vision, hollow.

She blinked at her vampire, but his eyes were closed. The veined misted shadows she loved stretched beneath his lashes, swaying over the tops of his cheekbones. His tongue swept over his bite as he sucked. The feigned sensation of his cock thrusted deeper and Faye squirmed, unable to escape her sweet torment.

"Rune please, I want you inside me," she breathed.

He opened his eyes but kept his mouth on her thigh. *You can tell us apart?*

"Of course, I can," Faye said with a moan. Rune lifted his head, and his phantom touch lowered her to the bed before dissipating.

He arched a brow. "Truly?"

Was he serious? Faye quirked her lip and sat up, mildly offended, he thought she viewed the two of them as interchangeable. He wasn't just a body to be occupied by whomever was available. She knew them both.

Loved them both.

She gently brushed his cheek and smiled. "If Voshki rose, he wouldn't be on his knees or tied up. And all of your ghost hands are kind of a giveaway, big guy."

Rune phased through the silk ropes and prowled over her. He conjured phantom hands to pin her wrists above her head. Faye's eyes widened and she sucked in a breath when he added a phantom mouth to tongue her pretty cunt.

"Your views please me, love," Rune purred. He wasn't the feared Shadow Prince or a vicious Pure Blood with her. She saw him as a man, one separate from the Ra'Voshnik.

And she was the woman he devoted his heart to, in its entirety.

She pulled against his phantom hold. "Stop teasing me. I need you."

Rune knew he shouldn't, but he thoroughly enjoyed her begging. "I could fuck you for hours and never touch you, vsenia."

The creature ran its claws over his awareness. *Bring her into our mind. I want to test her theory.*

Calm yourself, Rune grated.

He leaned closer, adding more sensations to his pleasure-fraught queen. Kisses trailed down her neck. His phantom teeth nipped her hip. Unseen fangs scraped the curve of her breasts as tongues lashed her tight nipples. "Do you want the Ra'Voshnik and I to take you, my queen? Do you need us both to satisfy your ache?"

Faye's back bowed off the bed and he cursed in High Tongue. He could come watching her writhe beneath his will.

Rune leaned back on his heels and unfastened his pants. His cock throbbed as he pulled himself free. Every vampiric instinct he possessed demanded he pin her beneath him and bury his cock and fangs in her yielding flesh. If he were a selfish lover, he may have surrendered to the desperate urgings. He held back, suspecting his dark queen wished to be bedded by himself and the Ra'Voshnik after they tended to her on his desk.

Confusion drifted from the creature. *You want her to ask to be fucked by both of us?*

I want her to trust me with her desires, Rune corrected. He wanted Faye to feel secure in her relationship with him and the Ra'Voshnik. He was aware she loved them both and while he did not understand what she favored in the creature, loving it did not negate her affection for him.

And if she wished to be fucked by them both... he and the Ra'Voshnik would happily see to her desires.

Rune hissed a breath as his cock met her delicate flesh. The head of his cock slid against her slick folds, and he rocked his hips. Faye moaned, panting as he dragged his length over her clit in calculated strokes. He mercilessly worked her lithe body and when she was breathless, he swept the head of his cock lower and nudged into her wet heat.

"Whose cock do you want stroking inside you, vsenia?"

"Please," Faye cried breathlessly.

"What are you begging for? Should I bring you into my mind, or should we stay?" Rune asked, inching deeper. He brushed the pad of his thumb over her full lips. "Do you want me to fuck your mouth?"

She whimpered so sweetly and parted her lips. Rune dipped his thumb into her mouth, and she sucked. "Who do you imagine in your mouth, vsenia? Do you want your Voshki to spend on your tongue?"

Rune leaned over her, withdrawing his hand to kiss her softly. Darkness, she felt divine. It took every shred of his control to tease her with shallow strokes instead of driving his entire length into her.

"Name your desire and you will have it," Rune murmured. His queen tossed her head in answer. He leaned closer and said in a firmer tone, "Say the words, love."

"Bring… bring me into your mind."

Rune carried her awareness into his and straightened before flipping her on to her stomach.

"Rune!" Faye cried in breathless surprise.

"Yes, my queen," he answered as he crossed her wrists behind her back and wrapped the silk rope over her forearms. She remained still as he pulled the soft material into matching loops and laced them higher.

"When did you learn this?" Faye asked over her shoulder.

He strung the column of rope together, binding her wrists. "Did you think I sat idly during your lessons?"

Rune smiled, recalling their first. The instructor hid it well, but he reeked of fear. Rune ignored it, choosing to focus on Faye and her eager happiness. She'd sat on his lap while knotting silk rope over his dress shirt. He'd been willing to take it off, but his queen had stiffened when he made mention of it. He'd been thankful she allowed him to remove his jacket and watched as she wrinkled his sleeve beyond repair. When she'd finished her intricate design, it covered his arm from wrist to bicep.

Her giddy excitement pleased him, and she'd recreated her lattice at the end of the evening when they were alone. The corner of Rune's mouth lifted with the memory. She'd been kind, granting him a boon by allowing him to strip from the waist up. Sparing an innocent shirt from the atrocities she committed on the first.

"Why are you daydreaming when our queen is in front of us?" the creature asked from the other end of the bed. It called the fur lined blindfold she'd purchased from Kayla's arsenal.

Faye would have seen it, but her attention remained fixed on him as he finished securing the simple knot. Rune tested the slack by sliding two fingers between the rope and her wrist. "Move your hands for me, love."

Faye rolled onto her side and twisted her wrists before wiggling her fingers. "Voshki is usually the one in a rush to tie me up."

"It's because we're more alike than he cares to admit," the Ra'Voshnik said as it gently picked her up and drew her closer. The creature purred as it gathered her hair and let her dark tresses tumble over the edge of the mattress. "Can you tell us apart if you can't see us?" it asked, holding the blindfold in front of her with two fingers.

Faye giggled. "The two of you are *very* different."

"I could be the Shadow Prince," it said with a shrug. The creature traced the curve of her breast with the backs of its black tipped claws and glanced his way. "My name is Rune. I'm so serious. I strangle my vampiric urges because I can't allow myself to feel anything enjoyable."

"Be silent," Rune said curtly.

The Ra'Voshnik chuckled and pulled the blindfold over Faye's eyes as it nipped her ear. "Do you want to be tended to or fucked, love?"

Faye laughed and wet her lips. "Surprise me."

Rune hooked the back of her knee with his arm and gripped Faye's hip, trapping his queen on her side. He leaned closer, forcing her leg higher, while he straddled the other. He shouldn't have drunk from her thigh. Her blood electrified his senses, emboldening desires he kept on a tight leash.

The scent of her blood and arousal intoxicated him. His gaze lowered between them, and his fangs sharpened at the sight of her spread and wet. Instinct rode him, demanding he dominate his prey.

He fought the urge to drive his considerable length into her and groaned. His mind seized on the breathy cries he would elicit from her sweet lips when he stretched her around his cock.

Darkness, how she would take it for him.

Rune rocked his hips, teasing her with the head of his cock. His back tensed as she squeezed him, and he cursed in High Tongue. The teasing pleasure was as torturous for him as it was for her.

Faye strained against her bonds and arched her back. "Rune, please."

"Open your mouth, vsenia. Swallow the Ra'Voshnik's spend, and I will make you come until I tire of hearing you scream my name."

His night breeze gazed up at the creature through the fur-lined mask and took its cock past her lips. The last time they'd been in this position, Faye had been on her hands and knees. Pinned on her side, Rune had a clear view of her bound and blindfolded while the creature fucked her mouth. It was easy with her, stroking half its length into her mouth in a lazy rhythm while she licked and sucked.

Rune often fantasized about fisting her hair and fucking her lovely throat but would never subject his queen to such base urges.

The creature tilted its chin back and groaned. "Suck harder, love." It gazed down at her and brushed the curve of its index over her cheek. "You're too gentle." Its breath hitched and it smiled. "Yes, like that."

Faye moaned around his cock and the Ra'Voshnik's shoulders went rigid. It tensed and hissed as it came with a growl before choking on a breath. Faye sucked harder while the creature came, and Rune chuckled. Vindictive minx.

She swallowed its spend and Rune thrusted his entire length into her as the Ra'Voshnik lowered to its knees beside the bed. It purred, wrapping her in its arms. Faye laid her head down, moaning with each of Rune's punishing thrusts.

The Ra'Voshnik teased Faye's nipples as it nuzzled her throat. "Do you like being tied and blindfolded? Helpless while the Shadow Prince fucks your pretty cunt?"

Rune purred at the intimate fluttering around his cock. His queen liked it when the creature spoke filth to her. There would be many nights to coax her proclivities from her. They had discovered enough this evening. Rune conjured a phantom mouth to purr on her clit as he took her in a harsh rhythm.

Faye screamed and tremored, coming around his cock. The Ra'Voshnik held her closer, kissing her throat. "Take it, vsenia."

Rune tensed, chasing his release. He fucked her harder. Panting his breaths. His cock twitched and he thrusted into her a final time, gripping her waist with bruising force. His chest heaved as he emptied himself deep inside her.

"Try coming like that when she's still sucking your cock," the Ra'Voshnik said with a laugh.

Rune's cock pulsed as he poured more of himself into her. The creature tugged off Faye's blindfold and untied the silk binding her wrists while Rune caught his breath. It rubbed her shoulder and his queen sighed, going limp between them.

"Should I draw you a bath, vsenia?" Rune asked as he kneaded the small of her back.

Faye moaned and shook her head once.

The Ra'Voshnik ran its fingers through her hair and said, "You could stay with me and tell the Shadow Prince to rub your feet."

Faye swatted the creature's arm and giggled. "Behave."

"Did you wish to soak in the gardens?" Rune asked. He always bathed her and washed her hair after their love making. An unspoken apology for his rough treatment.

"No," she said, untangling herself from the creature and sat up. Her eyes were heavy lidded, and her lips were swollen but a smile lit her lightning-streaked midnight eyes. She spoke three simple words and his cock hardened in an instant.

"I want more."

Beneath the Hunter's Moon

Takes place after A Trial of Lace and Bone.

Compulsive aggression and possessive impulses deteriorated Rune's calculated mind. The Hunter's Moon began its ascent and while the blood-red glow didn't bathe Hell beneath its ominous light, Rune *felt* it.

Faye stood before the full-length mirror in the corner of their room, clad in a gray lace lingerie set. She adjusted her straps and straightened the ribbons, unaware of his presence.

Rune stalked his unsuspecting prey, silently closing the distance between them. Faye adjusted her garter belt and pointed her toe to inspect the jewel encrusted heels she'd worn at the Artithian Princess's wedding. The corner of his mouth lifted when she lifted her gaze and startled. Rune seized on the dilation of her lightning-streaked eyes. The flush of adrenaline coloring her cheeks. Her racing heart.

Darkness, she made his cock hard.

He gripped the mirror's bloodroot frame on either side of her, trapping her between himself and the glass. He inched closer and

Faye retreated until her breath fogged her reflection. Faye held his mirrored stare and wet her lips.

"Does Morbid have the twins?"

A low growl vibrated through Rune's chest as he grappled with her words. Why was another man's name on her tongue when she belonged to him? His young were asleep in the adjacent nursery and Rune had every intention of fucking the Familiar King's name out of his luscious prey's vocabulary.

"Rune," she said in a sterner voice. "You need to take the twins to Morbid."

"Do I?" he rasped. He'd rather order her to hold the mirror while he gripped her hips and stretched her exquisite cunt over his cock.

Deliver my young to the Familiar King, Voshki growled through his mind. Rune returned his aggression and mentally turned inward, preparing to rend the rival for Faye's affection into bloody strips. *You will lose Shadow Prince. If you can't keep your mind about you, I'll imprison you and deliver my young, myself.*

Rune bared his fangs but fingertips against his wrist drew his attention. Faye traced circles over his tendons and leaned into the hard plains of his body. Rune purred, rubbing the side of his face in her dark hair. She wanted him. He could scent it on her. His night breeze through plum blossoms spiked with notes of her arousal.

She turned in the tight space of his arms and her wine-colored lips warmed his throat. She moved higher, trailing kisses along his jaw. The corner of his mouth.

"Please take our children to the Familiar King," she whispered quietly.

Her lips met his in a quiet kiss and he vaguely recalled needing to be still, but he couldn't rationalize why.

Faye broke the kiss but remained a breath away. She smoothed her hand down the side of his neck and said, "When you come back you can have me. I'll offer you my throat while you fuck me. You can have all of me *after* I know our children are safe."

His rational mind was a bothersome whisper, overwhelmed by the instincts raging through him. He would deliver his young into the arms of Chaos. They would be safe and then his little queen would submit to every urge he possessed.

Rune leaned in and smiled when she didn't pull away. "When I return you will be on my sheets with your legs spread, vsenia," he grated. The backs of his fingers travelled past her navel to the lace thong she wore. "And take these off, or I will rip them from your body."

Faye gave him a small nod and he stepped back.

Voshki's presence lingered at the edges of his mind but remained silent as Rune strolled into the nursery. He quickly gathered each bundle and phased to Chaos. To his surprise the Familiar King stood on the corner of the landing pad to his estate. Morbid took a step toward him and Rune bared his fangs instinctively. His queen spoke this male's name.

He should return to Faye with his severed head as a gift.

Morbid tsked at him and Rune's mind focused with predatorial intent. A carefree smile spread over the Familiar King's features, and he bowed in a small flourish.

"Now, now. You want me to watch your young so you can return to your queen," Morbid said, taking another step toward Rune and reaching for his son.

Easy, Voshki said softly through his mind.

Morbid collected his twins and stepped off the platform. "Good hunting, Prince. Your queen isn't in bed waiting for you," he said over his shoulder.

Rune's mind frenzied to Faye, and he phased back to his room. His four-post bed draped in dark silk came into sharp focus. His empty sheets revealing her betrayal. Rune's canines lengthened. His prey had fled.

The injuries he'd sustained in the Hall of Empty Eyes hindered his ability to wield the full depth of his power—but nothing could take Hell from him.

Rune reached for his realm, and it revealed Faye's location. She'd returned to their private gardens and his cock hardened as memories of when he'd chased her through the manicured, black rose hedges played behind his eyes.

There was no escaping him. When he captured her, he would use his realm to fuck her mouth, ass, and cunt, until she begged for mercy. The corner of his lips lifted.

A kindness he would not be granting.

Rune phased to his queen's hellfire-lit sanctuary. He material-ized from a burst of ash and shadows as blue embers burned to soot around him.

His gaze raked over Faye, and she smiled at him from the ornate canopy bed veiled in white organza. She crossed her arm in front of her as though he'd kept her waiting and squeezed her breasts togeth-er.

"This is not where I left you," he grated. "But I see you partially obeyed me."

His queen looked down at herself and spread her legs, giving him a better view of her pussy. "I couldn't have you ripping my pant-ies off me," Faye answered, as she closed her thighs.

Steam billowed from the hot spring and rolled past his queen as hellfire highlighted her dainty features. "There are consequences when you run from me," Rune rasped.

A mischievous gleam lit her lightning-streaked midnight eyes and her words bloomed through his mind. *You like to chase. I like to run.*

Faye leaned forward, tracing her ankle with the tip of her ma-roon nail before gliding higher, following the curve of her calf. Rune stared, transfixed as she traced her inner thigh and spread her legs. She flattened her palms on the bed and crisscrossed her wrists to hide her bare sex.

Her breaths slowed as she tensed to phase and Rune's fangs sharpened. She was a glorious sight, begging his vampiric instincts to pursue her. Rune would have his fiery queen on her knees with hollowed cheeks and teary lashes.

He stalked closer, intent on punishing her each time she fled. He conjured a phantom hand to palm the curve of Faye's ass. The corner of his mouth lifted when he directed it lower. She sucked in a breath and straightened her back when the oiled digit roughly fucked her ass.

Faye's gold-streaked eyes widened as she gasped, "Rune."

"I will be adding a finger each time you run from me, vsenia," he said, loosening his tie.

Faye stood on shaking legs and sauntered toward him, ignoring the flush creeping across her cheeks. She tugged his tie loose and let it fall as she palmed his cock. "I have no intention of laying down and spreading my legs for you, big guy. You'll need to catch me," she teased, staring up at him.

Rune's lashes lowered to the pout in her wine-colored lips. "Get on your knees and beg me to fuck your throat, vsenia."

"No," she breathed, running the heel of her palm down his shaft before promptly vanishing.

His instincts raged at the loss of his prey. Rune bared his fangs, extinguishing the lanterns with a flicker of his mind. He grinned, surveying his hunting ground. His kind saw perfectly in the dark, but his quarry would be hard pressed to navigate her surroundings by the subtle glow of the blood-red moon.

Faye appeared beside her garden and froze in the darkness. Rune moved in a blur, fisting the back of her hair as he stepped into her. She went rigid as a second phantom finger joined the first, thrusting in and out of her pretty ass.

"Rune," she cried, standing on her toes.

"Take it," Rune hissed as he tightened his grip on her hair and reduced her lingerie to shadows and whisps of ash. He suddenly pinned her against him, molding her soft curves to his muscled body. The scent of her arousal stripped him of logic and reason.

All he knew was she belonged to him, and he would possess her.

"There is no escaping me, love," he groaned, brushing the side of his face against hers in an animalistic caress. "Submit."

Pleasure lashed him as his little queen arched her back and ground her ass up and down the length of his cock.

"I'll submit when you *manage* to pin me," she breathed before vanished once more.

"Faye!" Rune bellowed.

His focus sharpened to a razor's edge as he scanned the manicured grounds. He reached for Hell and found his prey had resurfaced in their well-lit bedroom. He sealed his realm, restricting Faye's ability to phase through his reality.

Amusement thrummed from Voshki, but he remained a silent voyeur in the recesses of Rune's mind.

Rune stepped through his realm, materializing in his bedroom in a violent plume of shadows and ash. Faye stood beside their bed post flushed and panting as his will continued to fuck her. He prowled closer to his queen, adorned in the single article he'd left her.

A pair of jewel-encrusted black satin heels.

He stretched her to take another shadowy finger and conjured a phantom mouth to purr on her clit. She moaned, leaning heavily on the bedpost. A flush radiated down her throat and between her breasts. The minx arched her back, daring him to tie her hands and fuck her against the post.

"Keep running, vsenia." Rune closed the distance between them, dropping his voice an octave. "I could fuck you for hours without touching you, love."

And he would.

Faye lifted her chin in the defiant way he'd grown to relish, even as shallow pants slipped past her parted lips. He reached for her, and she dashed beside their bed, but Rune was faster. He caught her by the back of the neck, and she shrieked with laughter as he shoved her onto their bed.

Darkness blinded Faye and the steady pressure of Rune's hand caging the back of her neck pinned her firmly in place. The silk sheets wrinkled beneath the side of her face, and Faye kicked in an effort to right herself. She couldn't think with his phantom touch fucking her ass. Couldn't concentrate. Her struggles left her tangled in the sheets and Rune's dark chuckle swept over her skin.

He was too strong. She couldn't break free. Faye moaned, giving in to his illicit touch. He'd trapped her, and Darkness help her when he realized how wet their game made her.

Faye froze when his chest pressed flush to her back and his weight pressed her deeper into the mattress. The cashmere wool cooled her skin, making her painfully aware of the powerful, chiseled body beneath it.

"Must I remind you of what I am, vsenia? I do not rule Hell. I am Hell," he rasped.

Glimmering crystalline spikes rose from the ground beside the frost pink azaleas. The soil tumbled away in chunks as Hell's landscape invaded her picturesque garden, rising higher. It arched up creating a beautiful pergola, illuminating the hot spring and willows beside their bed.

Her surroundings flickered and the light gray sheets were replaced with grass. Rune phased them to the ground in the center of the crystalline structure. Ropes made of shadows and tumbling ash lashed from the posts, capturing her wrists and ankles. They curled up her limbs, tangling above her knees and elbows.

Faye struggled and hellfire shook from her restrains, bursting into hundreds of glimmering blue flecks, the same way embers tossed when she stoked a fire.

The pressure on her throat relented as a shadowed rope descended from the pergola's ceiling and circled her middle. It split, forking over her ribs before binding together beneath her. Her hell-made harness widened to spread over her hips and ended at the swell of her breasts.

Faye moaned when Rune's phantom touch withdrew from her ass. Her moment of calm was short lived, and she gasped when her restraints snapped, jerking her off the ground.

The band over her middle dictated the angle of her body while her arms and legs were immobilized by the shadowed ropes coiled over her forearms and shins. Faye's wrists were yanked behind her, and she tipped forward as her restraints pulled tight. Her legs were forced wide, and Rune possessively palmed the back of her thigh.

Faye let her head drop, glancing at her vampire upside down. The man was on his knees, somehow finding the time to strip between pinning her to their daybed and trussing her up. She admired his cock and bit the inside of her lip, silently wondering if he was going to angle her lower and fuck her throat like this. She took in the gorgeous lines of his chiseled body, following them higher and froze. His chest met his collarbone and vanished behind the junction of her thighs.

His face was inches from… everything!

A blistering flush radiated off Faye's cheeks and she hissed, "Rune."

"I could fuck you for hours without touching you, vsenia. Shall I demonstrate?"

He gripped the back of her thighs and squeezed her ass. Faye wiggled in his hold as his thumbs settled on either side of her pussy. He parted her silken flesh and purred darkly. "Look how wet you are, love."

Another pair of hands joined his and Faye doubled her efforts to escape as they spread her ass cheeks.

"You should not have run from me," her vampire mused.

Rune's firm lips brushed the edge of her cunt—through his thumbs holding her open as though they weren't there. Darkness, she was fucked. He'd injured his core and could only hold one phantom touch like Voshki for months.

But apparently her vampire was more resourceful under the strain of the Hunter's Moon, and decided his Hell-magic was a great solution.

"I am going to fuck you until you no longer have the strength to stand," he murmured lovingly.

Rune gripped the bend of her waist and tilted his head before slanting his mouth over her slit. He licked inside her and Faye whimpered. He pressed his face into her soft flesh and fucked her with his tongue.

It was only a tease, and the vampire dick knew it. She was too aroused after running from him. The tension coiling in her was wound tight and she desperately needed his cock moving inside her to relieve the ache.

She recalled how he'd tormented her last year and cried in a rush, "Rune, please fuck me. I want your cock in my pretty cunt."

He withdrew from her, and she felt him smile against her spread pussy. Faye went limp in her restraints. He would stand up and—

"No," Rune answered, interrupting her thoughts. "Beg me to fuck your ass."

His fingertip teased the entrance of her cunt. He pressed the tip inside her before adding another.

She moaned as he thrusted deeper. He scissored his fingers, stretching her and pleasure jolted through her nerve endings. Faye's breath caught in her throat, and she couldn't breathe. He curled his index, stroking the spot deep inside her and she tremored.

"Rune," Faye cried, flutily struggling against the restraints.

He chuckled and grazed his fangs along the back of her thigh before forcing her to take a third digit.

Faye arched her back, unknowingly giving him better access. He filled her completely, overwhelming her senses.

Something wide and blunt pressed against her ass and Faye's eyes snapped open. "I didn't beg you yet."

"And I am not fucking you yet," Rune answered.

Faye panted, fighting her bonds. The head of his shadowed cock slowly worked into her ass beneath his steady pressure.

"You will take everything I give you," he grated. "And beg for a great deal more."

The ropes spread her legs wider, and Rune circled her clit with his tongue.

"Rune, please. Purr for me. Let me come," Faye begged, rolling her hips.

"No," he answered before returning to her sweet torture.

He licked her clit each time his fingers slid into her cunt. Faye moaned breathlessly as he worked her with slow and deliberate thrusts. His hand gave her the satisfaction of being filled while simultaneously maddening her by intensifying the ache building between her legs.

He'd edged her viciously in the past, but it had been physical. Rune would take her to the very edge of her pleasure and stop before the tension in her snapped. He held her there until she writhed under him, begging him to let her come.

Tonight, he wrung pleasure from her body as well as her mind. She was bound and trapped, completely at her vampire's mercy. She couldn't escape him. Couldn't squirm away from the steady pressure of his shadowed cock in her ass.

It didn't fuck her the way Rune had in the past. He'd worked his length into her in increments, withdrawing and pressing deeper. This was drawn out and methodical. There was no withdrawal. No moment of relief before he pressed into her deeper. His shadowed cock was constant, forcing her gradual surrender as she took it deeper.

Rune was inescapable and his inevitability made her wetter than she'd ever been in her life.

Faye arched her back and begged, "Fuck me, Rune. Please fuck my pretty ass."

"Show me your wings, love," he countered.

"What?" Faye breathed.

Rune curled his fingers in answer, stroking the spot inside of her and Faye's mind blanked. She struggled, needing more. Darkness, she could come if he just pressed on her clit a little harder.

He kissed her there and teasingly flicked her with his tongue.

"Let me come, please," Faye cried, struggling helplessly.

"I want your wings, vsenia. Give them to me," Rune said in a darker tone.

Faye reconciled his words and closed her eyes. She welled her strength and it rose in a rush. The space between her shoulder blades heated and her nailbeds tingled as her magic fused with her body. Raw power erupted from her back, arching past her and Faye shifted under the weight of her iridescent wings.

"You are mine, vsenia," Rune said as he stood. "And I will have every part of you."

The phantom cock withdrew and Faye turned her head as far as Rune's restraints allowed, glancing back at her vampire.

A crimson glow bathed his silhouette, and tension riddled his muscular shoulders. He gripped her waist and thrusted into her ass the same moment shadows surrounded her.

Rune fucked her mercilessly as dozens of shadowed hands and mouths roamed her body. His Hell-shadows alternated between roughly tugging on her nipples and sucking on the hard peaks with a hint of teeth.

"Look at me, vsenia. I want to see your eyes when you come," Rune commanded.

Faye met his gaze and stared. His veins stood out against his forearms as his chiseled muscles flexed with each possessive thrust.

"Good girl," Rune crooned with a vicious smile.

A phantom mouth purred against her clit and Faye tensed. She blinked, holding Rune's stare, afraid he would stop if she closed her eyes.

"Please, Rune. Fuck me harder. Let me come," she pleaded desperately.

"Open your wings," he rasped.

Faye immediately obeyed him, and Rune traced circles on the inside of her wing where the membrane met her back. She struggled to keep her eyes on Rune as the tension coiling within her finally snapped. Pleasure crashed through her in waves, and Faye screamed her release, coming hard.

She came down, panting as bliss began raining through her body.

Rune chuckled, roughening the purr on her clit. Faye's muscles seized as she tensed before coming again.

"Look at me, vsenia," Rune warned.

Faye held his gaze while he wrung orgasm after orgasm from her. She begged for mercy during the first six and could scarcely form words after the fourteenth. She'd lost count of how many times she came and when Rune finally relented, she was covered in a sheen of perspiration.

Faye went limp, sagging against her bonds. She wasn't sure when the little cloud of shadows and ash pillowed the side of her head, but she was grateful for Rune's small mercy.

She rested against it, dimly aware of the purr rumbling from Rune's chest. He increased his pace and she blinked, obediently watching him fuck her. His eyes hardened as he used her body to chase his pleasure. Her hair swayed over the grass as he took her in a hard, desperate rhythm.

The sight was so erotic Faye nearly came again.

Rune bared his fangs, thrusting into her a final time. His cock pulsed as he came, and Faye smiled. Completely exhausted and unable to do anything else.

Faye moaned breathlessly as Rune withdrew. He gathered her in his arms and the shadowed restraints became less tangible and vanished. They reminded Faye of her own wings, and she wiggled in Rune's hold. His arm was flushed to her back, and she couldn't remember when her wings faded. *Probably before he made her a shadow pillow*, Faye mused to herself.

Rune lowered them into the hot spring, and she closed her eyes. She welcomed the heat, letting it ease her stiff muscles. Her vampire washed away the remnant of his intense lovemaking and a pleasant chime sounded.

Faye peeked over his shoulder, curious.

A tray balanced on the pool's stone border. Glasses of water, pomegranate juice, and tea were arranged with small plates piled with sugar-coated strawberries, choice cuts, and almond cookies. Faye smiled knowing this was Voshki's doing.

Rune lifted her out of the steaming water and took a seat beside the snacks.

He pulled the refreshments closer and swept Faye's hair behind her shoulder. He nuzzled her throat and murmured, "Drink. After you quench your thirst, I want you on your knees. You will spread your legs and beg me to fuck your cunt and ass with Hell's will."

Faye leaned into him and reached for the glass of water. "Will I?" she asked.

His fingers seductively closed over her slim neck. "After I am through fucking this pretty throat, I will stretch your exquisite cunt around my cock."

Faye smiled at their game. She sipped her water and exposed her throat while admiring the willow trees framing the hot spring.

"And after that?" she asked.

Her vampire pulled her closer and whispered softly, promising the tone for the rest of her evening.

"You will submit to my fangs and beg for my cock while my shadows ravage you. I intend to make you come for hours and when you are certain you could not possibly take anymore… You will."

MARK ME

Leather slid against a cool metal buckle and a chill whispered over Faye's skin. She arched her back, glancing behind her. Veined misted shadows swayed beneath Voshki's dark gaze as a small shiver went through her. He fastened a finely crafted black leather cuff over her wrist. A twin to the first, connected behind her back by three shining chain links. Her beautiful hunter sat at the edge of their bed. Lengths of his long white-blonde hair fell across the hard plains of his chest. He leaned closer, brushing his lips over her shoulder.

"Comfortable?" he purred.

Faye wiggled, testing her range of motion. The lining was soft, cushioning her wrist while keeping her restrained. "Yes," she said, leaning toward him. She stopped a moment from his lips and pulled back. "How many of these do you have?" He used two others to tie her down the last time she met him alone. The time before that—

Faye's cheeks heated. They were the first set of restraints he brought her. Crimson leather lined with black satin. He'd bound her wrists in front of her and wound a silk sash around the chain. She'd been confused when he looped the sash around the bedpost but understood after he pinned her beneath him. He pulled the length of silk, keeping her arms taut above her head the entire night.

He'd introduced her to small metal clips with dainty silver bells attached to them. They pinched her nipples, and she'd grown more sensitive the longer she wore them. Voshki had conjured a phantom mouth to lick and purr against her clit, while he'd teased her with the tip of his cock. It wasn't long before she was desperate, begging him to fuck her.

She quietly wondered what he planned for her tonight and lightly bit the inside of her lip. She dragged it through her teeth, imagining the things she would do to him when it was her turn. Voshki maneuvered her onto her back and smoothed her hair over the edge of the bed.

Excitement thrummed in her, vibrating beneath her skin. She gazed up at him as he stood, admiring the way his chiseled muscles twisted and flexed with his movements. He'd already stripped out of his buttoned shirt, wearing only dress slacks.

Voshki stood at the end of the bed, regarding her upside down in her view. He hooked his finger under the strap of her bra, caressing higher as he admired the lingerie he'd chosen for the evening. He traced the boning stitched into the strips of black leather covering the swell of her breasts.

"You are so beautiful," Voshki said, brushing his fingertips along the edge of her lingerie collar. Faye sighed, closing her eyes. He wasn't always gentle, but when he was…

Faye thought back to the first night she spent with him. How she'd expected their first evening to mirror her ceremony of blood, but his only concern had been what *she* wanted. He'd held her close and filled their evening with conversation. How he'd longed for her and would worship her for the rest of his days. He never demanded, never pressured her into giving anything she didn't willingly submit. He treasured her and the absolute certainty he offered made heat pool at her center.

Voshki's touch brought her mind back to the present. He followed the strap of black leather to the back of her neck and rasped, "Your stockings are in the way."

Faye blinked. How were her stockings in the way? None of the collars he bought her included panties or even a thong. She narrowed her eyes at him and said, "My stockings are fine."

"I might have you wear them later," he teased, unfastening the collar. Faye swallowed as what little she had been wearing vanished.

"Spread your legs, vsenia," Voshki purred.

Faye's breaths turned shallow as she obeyed. He kissed her softly and moved lower, nipping her collarbone. The mattress sank under her waist as he leaned over her. Strands of his long white-blonde hair fell against her, cool on her skin. Sliding over her breasts and down her stomach as he crept over her body.

Faye sighed as fingers glided through her folds. He spread her open and groaned, holding her exposed to his view. "Look how wet you are for me, love."

The tops of her ears heated, and Faye squirmed under his scrutiny. "Voshki, please."

He purred, kissing her clit before slowly licking her silken flesh. Her toes curled as he pressed his tongue into her. She rolled her hips with each suck and lick, moaning his name.

Voshki pulled back and Faye whimpered, needing him inside her. He slipped a hand under her ass and rolled onto his back, taking her with him.

"Voshki!" Faye cried, shaking as he pulled her down on his mouth. She instinctively sat up and he drew her back, spreading her legs until she rested against him.

Lean back, love. You won't hurt me, Voshki promised.

Faye tentatively rocked, taking his tongue deeper.

You taste divine, Voshki groaned. He fisted the chain between her wrists as his other hand tangled in her dark hair.

Faye let him guide her down, and his purr filled her mind. He released her tress to unfasten his pants.

Open your mouth, he growled.

A thrill slipped down her spine, and Faye took his cock past her lips. He tilted his waist, fucking her mouth with slow strokes.

Faye moaned, opening wider. She licked and sucked the way Rune had taught her for the Hunter's Moon.

The next time you're with me and the Shadow Prince, you can suck his cock and sit on my face, Voshki teased.

An image filled her mind. Voshki was on his back between the settee and the smoked marble fireplace in Rune's study. She straddled his face while Rune stood before her. Voshki's black tipped claws teased her nipples and Rune fisted her hair, thrusting his entire length past her lips.

Faye tensed. The feel of his mouth and the illicit scene Voshki played were too much. She moaned around his cock as she came, and he lifted her hips. She cried out, and before she could beg him to continue, a phantom hand roughly drove two fingers inside her.

Bliss rained into euphoria.

Voshki's lips brushed her inner thigh. He kissed her once, then sank his fangs deep.

Ecstasy crashed through her, and Faye came again. She tried to sit up, but Voshki barred his arm across her back. Pleasure over-whelmed her, paralyzing her, and Voshki held her at his mercy. Fuck-ing her mouth.

The shadowed fingers withdrew and pressed into her again, slower. *Three?* Faye moaned helplessly around his cock as he stretched her, thrusting deeper.

She closed her eyes in surrender. Her mind drifted, and she con-centrated on the feel of her vampire. Voshki stroked into her mouth, pressing further each time until he began fucking her throat.

You're such a good girl. Taking my cock so well, Voshki purred. A soft touch accompanied his praise and Faye sighed as his fingertips brushed her hollowed cheek.

She'd lost count of how many times she came when he released her. Faye curled on to her side, breathless and spent. Her lips swollen from his use.

Voshki crawled over her and kissed her softly. She nipped his throat and quickly bit down. Voshki laughed playfully through her mind.

Harder, vsenia. Mark me.

Voshki pinned her waist, thrusting into her mercilessly. Her moan skimmed over his neck, and she bit down harder. He growled ap-preciatively, withdrawing his cock to the tip before driving his entire length into her wet heat.

Darkness, her touch electrified his senses, drowning him in a torrent of sensations he never wanted to escape. He needed her spread beneath him, breathless, and begging.

Voshki forced her legs apart, each of his punishing thrusts jarring her lithe body. Instincts rode him, demanding her possession. He took her throat, sinking his fangs deep.

Faye screamed around her bite as her tantalizing blood coated his tongue. Voshki lost himself in the taste of her. It was exquisite, laced with the Darkness itself.

You have a vampire's instincts, Voshki purred through her mind as he savored her taste. *Would you like to know what you're saying, vsenia?* His queen moaned and Voshki grinned. *A vampire's bite is a show of dominance. Your teeth on my throat mean you want me to show you who will master you. You're asking me to mercilessly fuck your pretty cunt until you submit. You'll release your bite and spread your legs for my cock. Is that what you want?* Voshki asked, not missing a stroke.

Yes, untie me, Faye answered with a breathless sigh.

Voshki vanished the restraints and Faye dug her nails into his back, biting harder. He groaned low in his throat, not bothering to slow his brutal tempo as she came, squeezing his length intimately.

Darkness, she was made for him—aggressive and so fucking perfect.

Her lips closed over her bite and Voshki exhaled a shaky breath. His fangs sharpened as she dragged her tongue over his throat while she sucked.

His queen encompassed his being. The sensual feel of her mouth, the intoxicating taste of her blood, and the way she trembled beneath him as she came.

Faye released her bite, and his name slipped past her lips in a breathless sigh. An approving growl rumbled through him, but he was far from done with her. He fucked her harder, adding a phantom mouth to suck and purr on her clit.

"Voshki," Faye cried, gripping his shoulder.

He chuckled, kissing the blood from her neck. "Did you think this ended when you let go? Oh, vsenia, you're fated to a Pure Blood. We are viciously possessive creatures. Submitting doesn't mean I've mastered you. You're mastered when I've tested your submission to my satisfaction."

Voshki pinned her waist, rocking his hips at the end of each thrust. Teasing the sensitive spot deep inside her until she came apart.

"I can only hold one phantom touch at a time. You should be glad the Shadow Prince has a gentle temperament with you," Voshki said, roughening the purr on Faye's clit. His queen trembled beneath him, helplessly pinned while he drove her pleasure. "Or would you like that, vsenia? Having a dozen shadowed hands and mouths teasing you?"

Faye drew a shaking breath as she shuttered and Voshki's lips curled in an arrogant smile. He leaned closer, rasping in a hushed whisper, "Licking and sucking. Pressing into you. Should I invite him to join us, my queen? He would love to stretch your arms over your head… until you're standing on your toes. Has he fucked you with his will yet? Do you want his phantom cock in your pretty cunt?"

She hooked her arm over his neck suddenly, clinging to him as she lifted her back off the bed. Her iridescent wings flared past her shoulders, scraping over their silk sheets.

Voshki slowed his thrusts, stroking into her gently as he guided her thighs over his lean waist. He sat back on his heels, lifting Faye with him. She held him weakly as her panting breaths caressed his neck.

Voshki traced down her arm. He brought her hand to his lips and pressed a kiss to her palm before trailing lower. "Open your wings," he said before lightly dragging his teeth over her wrist.

Faye outstretched her shimmering wings, and Voshki delighted in her obedience. His night breeze couldn't please him more. He pricked her with a fang and closed his eyes, drinking her as he eased her back. Her dark hair and wingtips rhythmically swayed over their sheets as he took her in a harsh rhythm.

Voshki caressed the side of her face, dragging a black tipped claw over her lips. She licked the tip and opened for him. Letting him take from her.

"Fuck," Voshki cursed. His shoulders tensed and he pulled her to him, needing to feel her soft curves molded against him. He held her tighter, fisting her hair as he sank his fangs into her throat. The taste of her saturated his senses.

He chased his desperate need for her, gripping her waist with bruising force. His brows knit together, and Voshki came with a growl. Pleasure lashed him as he emptied more of himself into her.

"I will never have enough of you, vsenia," Voshki said as he caught his breath.

Faye folded her wings around him, enveloping him in their warmth as she ran her fingers through his hair.

"We have all night."

INSCRIPTIONS

Takes place after A Trial of Lace and Bone.

Muted beams of sunlight glimmered through the branches of a flowering plum tree overhead, showering Faye's private garden in a soft morning light. Rune joined Faye for a quiet brunch with her sister and Vashien after he'd taken Kae and Ren to Morbid earlier this morning.

Faye had longed for a family when she was young. The far-fetched dream of an orphaned Anarian girl, but in her musings, her family never consisted of powerful immortals. Faye smiled to herself. She'd never imagined the Familiar King would sulk if he wasn't allowed to babysit at least once a week.

She'd grown more comfortable as the months passed, her anxiety calming when her twins were out of her sight and protection. Morbid promised to protect her children as viciously as she would. *And,* Faye reminded herself, *Chaos was a closed realm after all.*

Life had become quiet since purging the Court of Lace and Bone. Kimber was adjusting to her new life as a vampire, Sparrow's immortality had finally set, and Faye ruled Anaria unopposed. She was happy, sharing her favorite meal with the people she loved.

Arranged over the decorative outdoor table constructed of metal and glass were several bamboo steamers containing dumplings and meats. Faye reached for a plate as Rune poured her tea. She smiled up at him, brushing his thigh in thanks.

Sparrow snorted and groaned loudly. "You two are nauseating," she said, dragging out the syllables.

Faye rolled her eyes and drizzled sweet soy sauce over her shrimp wrapped in a wide rice noodle. Her sister unceremoniously stuffed a pork dumpling in her mouth and Faye quirked her lip. "And you're still eating."

"I didn't say the food was bad. I said you two love birds are sickening," Sparrow clarified, emptying a steamer of shrimp dumplings onto her plate. She glanced at Vash as she peeled the shrimp out of their translucent wrappers. "And we need our own hot spring."

"Do we?" Vash asked over his mug of steaming coffee.

Sparrow huffed a breath and Faye laughed quietly. Her sister's shoulders fell, and she gave Vash her best pair of sad eyes. "How am I supposed to relax when Runey's bed is right next to the spring?" Sparrow whined, pointing to the gauzy canopy bed beside the white-furred stone rabbit's shrine.

There was no hot spring here, but Faye knew her sister referred to Rune's private gardens in Hell. The bed's twin was nestled in the shade of two willow trees beside the heated pool.

"His shadowy highness probably bends Faye over where I like to sit, too," Sparrow grumbled.

Faye studied her breakfast, refusing to comment on her sister's assumptions. Rune rarely bent her over. Lately her vampire was prone to spreading her legs and worshiping at her altar in his gardens or demanding she ride him, sinking his fangs into her throat as he lifted them out of the hot spring.

"Behave, or I'll drop you in a lake, sunshine," Vashien said, sipping his coffee.

Sparrow gave a soft hiss and pulled her plate closer.

"Take one of the rooms with an adjoining green space and have a private hot spring installed," Faye said.

Sparrow fell back in her chair and glanced up dramatically. "But I just finished unpacking." When Faye didn't reply Sparrow muttered, "Fine." She finished the dumpling's shrimp filling and emptied the discarded wrappers onto a nearby plate. "When are you getting married?"

Faye glanced at Vashien for help, but the traitor raised his brows and looked away. "Don't you get tired of asking?"

"Don't you get tired of deflecting?"

Faye absently adjusted her teacup. She planned to visit the same jeweler Rune purchased her engagement ring from. They had paid the shop for a lone meeting in the afternoon because her vampire wanted privacy. A compromise, since Faye didn't want to force the jeweler to close his shop and travel with all his goods for a viewing in Hell.

"I don't want to rush things," she said finally.

Sparrow stilled, holding a serving of dumplings over her plate, and blinked. "You said it had to wait until your realm was settled. It's *settled*, bitch. What are you waiting for?"

"I'm going to pay Vash to drop you in a lake," Faye said sweetly as she took a bite of her breakfast.

Sparrow fluttered her hand at her. "You can't have cold feet. You had babies with the man."

Faye could only imagine the level of hyper fixation Sparrow would reach when she got to plan her own wedding and stole a sympathetic glance at Vash. The poor man was in for it when he finally popped the question. Rune had told her their proposal derailed Vashien's, but he planned to surprise Sparrow during the New Year's Festival.

"Weddings take time," Faye said.

Sparrow made an exasperated noise and stared up into the morning sky. "No, they don't. It's a big party, you're over thinking it." Her sister instantly brightened and clapped her hands. "I could whip it all together in two weeks."

"No," Faye said firmly. She could hire a team of coordinators to arrange her wedding into an elaborate event the realms would talk about for years to come, but it wasn't what Faye wanted. She needed time to plan her wedding… and think of a way to include Voshki. He had loved her even when she was at odds with Rune. When she had no power.

When she was a simple Anarian.

She wanted him to know how much it meant to her. How much he meant to her.

"We're going to wait until Kae and Ren are two," Faye said, silently hoping it was enough time for her to interlace her and Rune's traditions while also including Voshki.

"That's more than a year away," Sparrow said. Her mouth slackened as her attention shifted to Rune, then Faye, and back to Rune. "Don't you want to be her husband now?"

Rune smirked. "I am the will of my queen."

"Of course, you are," Sparrow huffed.

Faye learned to manage her sister's insatiable curiosity when they were girls by offering up small details. It let Sparrow feel involved and allowed Faye some privacy. "We're going to look at wedding bands today."

Sparrow's green eyes glittered, and she straightened her back.

Vash snapped his wing around her chair and dragged her beside him. "You're not going with them."

Sparrow leaned heavily on his shoulder. "I better be invited when you go dress shopping."

They finished their meal and Faye said her goodbyes as Rune phased them to Necromia. A large room with dark gray walls came into focus. Rows of glass display cases were arranged throughout the space, but it was the hellfire chandeliers sparkling overhead that stole Faye's breath. Hundreds of tiny blue flames flickered above them, catching the facets of the jewels displayed below.

Faye held out her hand and tilted her engagement ring. It glittered more than she'd ever seen, from green to purple and back again.

"Shadow Prince. Queen Faye. I am honored to have you in my quaint establishment. May I offer you some refreshments?" A well-dressed man asked. Beside him a man and a woman in matching uniforms held two trays. One held a variety of pastries and the other a dozen glasses in a rainbow of hues.

"I'm fine but thank you for the offer," Faye said to the jeweler before smiling at the man and woman. She would never get used to how dark-bloods couldn't seem to shop without the extravagant snacks they called refreshments.

The waiters nervously glanced toward Rune and when he inclined his head, they retreated to the far end of the room. Faye leaned closer to her vampire, intertwining his fingers with hers. The pair stood as far from Rune as possible, and she suppressed her smile. While most gave her vampire a wide berth, this was an improvement. Definitely a far cry from her village's initial reaction to him.

"My name is Gregory. The Shadow Prince mentioned you would like to view our wedding bands," the jeweler said. At Faye's nod he gestured to a row of display cases behind him. "Just this way, my Lady."

Faye followed him and slowed to a stop as they passed the second glass case. Her heart raced as she stared at the silver and gold ear cuffs. "I didn't know you sold these," she said, gently brushing her fingers over the decorative curved metal.

Anarians often used ear cuffs in place of wedding bands. The cost of jeweled rings and affording a handfasting within a blood temple were beyond the means of many of her people.

Gregory smiled warmly and said, "The ear cuffs grew popular among the ladies who didn't want rings competing with the soul shard they displayed. I believe it comes from a custom in your realm."

Faye would never have believed Necromians would adopt Anarian traditions. She picked up a dainty gold cuff with a small, beveled edge.

"Do they inscribe their partner's name inside the band?" she asked.

"They do," he said. A slender metal stick appeared in his hand, and he twirled it once before saying, "I procured a spelled pen so they can write the name of their heart in their own hand."

Faye selected the wider band meant as the counterpart to hers before leaning back onto Rune and gazing up at him with a smile. "Would you wear an ear cuff?"

Rune silently observed the quickening beat of his queen's heart. Her excitement made his soul easy. Her happiness and contentment filled him with a sense of satisfaction he couldn't describe.

Voshki brushed the surface of his awareness, seizing on the gold cuff Faye rolled between her fingers. *Say yes,* Voshki purred.

"I would gladly follow any tradition you wish," Rune said.

Faye perused Gregory's offerings, scrutinizing each cuff over the three tables. She settled on two pairs and placed them on a black cloth before leaning into him and asking in a low tone, "Which one do you like better?"

Rune studied his queen's selection. They were simple bands, one gold and the other silver. Rune tapped his finger beside the golden cuffs. The metal would complement Faye's sun-kissed skin.

"Can we have this set, please?" Faye asked.

"Of course," Gregory answered. He placed a raised tray over the other cuffs and carefully arranged the polished metal on the black silk. "Will you be inscribing your names today?"

"Yes, thank you," Faye said, inching closer.

Rune smoothed his hand down Faye's back. She thrummed with excitement and leaned into him, hugging his arm.

If this is an Anarian marriage custom we should give her an Anarian wedding night, Voshki said as his imaginings surfaced in Rune's mind. A scene in their room played. Voshki pinned Faye to their bed by her throat. She lay face down with her legs spread wide. Voshki took her in a brutal rhythm as he brushed his lips over the golden cuff low on her ear.

Rune dispelled the images as Gregory straightened the curved metal and set them beside the spelled engraver.

"Let me know when you've finished the names. You can save them for a blood priest to install or I can do the piercing for you here."

Faye picked up the pen and stilled. The joy he'd seen in her ebbed as her shoulders fell. *Are you well, vsenia?* Rune asked directly to her mind.

Voshki reached for their queen, enveloping her consciousness with his own before gently asking, *What's wrong, love?*

Faye glanced at the other cuffs before her gaze returned to the straightened metal. *I can't fit both of your names on this.*

Voshki answered on the heels of her statement. *Inscribe the Shadow Prince on your ring and my name on your ear cuff.*

Rune knew Voshki was far from selfless in his suggestion, but he also recognized Faye's strain anytime the blonde harpy brought up their wedding plans. His queen was kindhearted and was struggling to find ways to include Voshki. Tonight, he would set her mind to ease and tell her Voshki would be present during their wedding ceremony.

Maybe we should just do rings. Both of your names will fit in the band, she said quietly.

The sadness tinging Faye's words pained him as sharply as a dagger between his ribs. *Write Voshki's name in the cuff, vsenia. It will ease your heart.*

Finally admitting she prefers me to you?

Rune's scalp stung and the corner of his mouth lifted. Faye must have tugged on a length of Voshki's hair.

He's being nice, Faye hissed. *Behave.*

Yes, my queen, Voshki muttered begrudgingly.

Faye leaned back and looked up at him. "Are you sure this is okay? We can do rings. I don't need ear cuffs."

"I am honored to follow your traditions," Rune said before adding, *and if Voshki has a tie to you, perhaps he will become less obnoxious.*

Trade places with me and I'll have the demeanor of a kitten, Voshki replied.

Do not give me reason to regret this, Rune warned Voshki as he receded. *Write her name in your cuff.*

Veined misted shadows stretched beneath Rune's gaze as Voshki came to the fore. He purred, stepping into Faye. She blinked up at him, her lightning-streaked midnight eyes wide. Rune had never allowed Voshki to rise in public, but they were isolated, and this was as good a time as any to gage Voshki's reactions.

The Ra'Voshnik trapped Faye, caging her with his body against the display case and placing a hand on either side of her. He leaned forward, deliberately pressing his chest into her back as he picked up the engraving tool and brought the larger cuff closer.

"Wear my name for me," Voshki purred in a low tone. He kissed her temple and inscribed 'vsenia' in High Tongue on the cuff he would wear. Pleased with himself, he drew the smaller cuff to Faye and twirled the thin metal tool in front of her.

Faye took the engraving tool and Voshki leaned closer, nipping the top of her ear. "I can't wait to kiss your new ornament while my cock is inside you."

"Stop." Faye laughed, pushing her shoulder against Voshki's chest. He leaned back but kept his hands on the counter on either side of her.

Their queen wrote Voshki's name in her elegant script and turned to catch Gregory's attention. The jeweler didn't question the inscriptions and to his credit he recovered quickly under Voshki's gaze.

Faye took a seat first and Gregory fastened the cuff to Faye's ear. She adjusted the cuff's position to the outer edge of her ear before the cartilage met her earlobe. After inspecting her reflection in a handheld mirror, she set it on her lap and sat up straighter. "This is where I would like it."

"Of course, Lady," Gregory said. "You'll feel some heat and a little pressure."

After a few moments he stepped back and Faye beamed, gingerly touching the ear cuff as she admired it in the mirror. "Thank you," she said, getting up from the chair.

Voshki took a seat and Gregory closed the jewelry over his ear. "If you wanted to make any adjustments, Shadow Prince," he said, holding the mirror out to Voshki. His hand remained steady even though his heart raced.

Do not antagonize him. Faye prefers his designs, Rune said in his mind.

He's been respectful to Faye, so I'll leave his head attached to his body, Voshki said before looking past Gregory to his queen. "How would you have me, love?"

Faye stood beside him and swept his hair behind his ear. She moved the cuff and Voshki closed his eyes, leaning into her touch. She giggled and straightened his head. "You're worse than a cat. Hold still."

Rune chuckled as Faye adjusted the cuff then leaned back on her heels before making another small alteration. Their new jewelry was displayed on the same side when they faced each other. Her right to his left. He relished carrying her markings.

He belonged to her… body and soul.

"There. I think that looks right," Faye said, brushing her fingertips over the side of Voshki's throat.

Gregory nervously stepped beside Faye, but Voshki didn't avert his eyes, keeping his dark gaze trained on his queen. Warmth swept over his ear and into the joint of his jaw. Magic sliced away a thin strip of cartilage and the metal slid through Voshki's ear.

The jeweler stepped back and smiled at Faye. "You two make

a wonderful pair. If you would like any other adjustments, I have a healer who assists me from noon to four each day."

Faye touched the cuff. "I think they're perfect. Thank you so much."

Voshki stood and inclined his head at Gregory. "Thank you," he said before taking Faye's hand. "Shall we, my queen?"

She smiled up at him and nodded. Their surroundings faded and they appeared on the walkway to Faye's private gardens. Sunlight gleamed through the pillars outside their family wing. Roses climbed the pillars, their red blooms scenting the air with their sweet fragrance.

Voshki drew Faye into his arms and Rune mirrored Voshki's contentment. They had a queen who loved and accepted them. Who owned them without fear... without hesitation.

Voshki tangled his fingers through Faye's dark hair and pressed his lips to her forehead. "I love you," he murmured before receding.

Rune regained control of his body and held Faye tighter. With Voshki at the fore, he experienced everything the body did, but it was hollow, like a phantom touch. When he was in control of his body, he could tangibly feel her in his arms. The warmth of her body. Her scent.

Things he took for granted. Nuances the Ra'Voshnik lived without.

Voshki floated peacefully through his mind. *You could share the body with me.*

Rune contemplated Voshki's request and said, *You will need to learn to behave as I do in public. To onlookers we are the same person.*

Voshki laughed. *Pretending to be you is simple. You treat everything like formal court or stare at people disapprovingly until they scurry away.*

Rune didn't reply. This would take time. He brushed Faye's hair behind her ear, admiring the golden cuff. She'd changed considerably from the Anarian mortal he'd first abducted. She wore an embroidered gown with a matching cloak to keep the chill at bay. Through their short time together she had changed him as well and taught him much.

"I did not think such a small trinket would affect me so deeply," Rune said quietly.

Remember it's my name she wears, Voshki snickered.

"Careful," Faye teased, leaning back while she straightened his lapel. She smoothed her hand over his chest and met his gaze. "People might think you care about mortal traditions."

"I care for my little…" Rune's brow drew down. "Should I call you wife now, vsenia?"

My wife, Voshki corrected.

A slow blush crept over Faye's cheeks. "We're Anarian married like we're dark-blood married. We'll be husband and wife after we kneel in a blood temple."

"I plan on kneeling for you many times before then," Rune purred.

Faye took his hand and led him toward the halls leading to their private rooms. "There's a lot to plan. A year isn't very long."

"I believe I can make the process a touch smoother," Rune said.

They entered their room and Rune took a seat at the edge of their bed. The sunlight and plaster walls kept his unwanted memories at bay. Memories that faded each day he spent in his queen's company.

Faye came to stand between his knees, and he settled his hands on her hips. She leaned in and her lips met his. Soft and inviting. "I appreciate you wanting to help with the wedding, but you'd scare the vendors," Faye whispered.

"Likely," Rune said with a grin. "I would speak of our wedding ceremony. Voshki will be present so you may stop vexing your mind on ways to include him. Your Voshki will be present."

Faye's lips parted and she blinked at him. Frozen. Mildly insulted by her silence, he canted his head.

"Does this not please you, vsenia?" he asked.

"I… No…" Faye stumbled through her words before blurting out, "How did he get you to agree to that?"

Rune chuckled and smoothed his palm down her arm. "We struck a bargain. He ensures your safety during the Hunter's Moon and in exchange he will be present for our wedding ceremony."

"You came to an agreement?" Faye asked, her tone disbelieving.

Rune hummed in answer and unclasped the collar of her cloak. It pooled on the marble floor and Rune slowly dragged the zipper of her dress down her back.

Faye tucked his hair behind his ear and traced the edge, stopping at the golden band. She smiled coyly and asked, "Are you planning on holding me down and fucking me while you kiss my ear cuff?" Rune narrowed his eyes a fraction and Faye said, "Voshki shows me every fantasy he has."

"Noted," Rune muttered.

Don't sulk. I don't tell her yours. Well, not all of them, Voshki snickered.

"I thought you two would want the same thing," Faye said, shrugging out of her gown.

The scent of her arousal intoxicated him. Rune's gaze fell to her high breasts before lowering to the flare of her hips. He admired her curves, fighting the vampiric instinct to pin her beneath him and drive his cock into her pretty cunt.

He swallowed as his fangs lengthened, tracing his fingertips over her thigh. He adored her new curves and wanted his mouth on every part of her. *I am claiming my evening with Faye,* he said through his mind.

Voshki didn't reply and floated through his mind as though he were merely observing.

"We have different predilections," Rune crooned. He stripped off his jacket and discarded it along with his shirt.

Faye unfastened his pants and pulled his length free. "What would my vampire like?" she asked, stroking his cock.

"Whatever my queen wishes," he groaned before leaning back on his hands. She fisted his cock, moving up and down as he watched. The minx's touch was too gentle and light. Rune exhaled, closing his eyes. Pleasure lashed through him, and his fangs ached. He needed her throat. Her blood on his tongue.

The mattress shifted as she crawled onto the bed with him, the silken skin of her inner thighs sliding against his waist.

"I want to know what you want," Faye breathed. Rune's breath hitched when the warmth of her mouth met the side of his neck. She lowered herself on his cock, taking the head and teasingly rolling her hips. "Should I bite your neck and run from you? You could catch me and fuck me like you do during the Hunter's Moon."

Rune sat up, capturing her against him and forcing her legs apart. He thrust several inches into her, pulling back only to drive his cock deeper. Her soft cries were muffled against his throat while he fucked her.

When she'd taken all of his considerable length, Rune pinned her waist against him. He palmed the curve of her ass and reached lower. Faye gasped and squirmed as he stroked her delicate flesh stretched around his cock.

"I would have you come a few times first, but I could add a finger," Rune purred as he teased the edge of her cunt. "Tease the spot you favor while I fuck you."

A breathy moan slipped past her lips as he added a bit of pressure. "I can't," Faye breathed. "You're too big."

"I could tease your ass," Rune said. Her desire coated his fingers, and he moved higher. Circling. "Would you like me to fuck you here? Make you writhe on my cock until you make me come, vsenia. Or did you want me to be gentle?" He leaned closer, his breath caressing the curve of her ear. His lips brushed the cuff. "Would my queen prefer I kiss her nipples and take her slow?"

Faye turned toward him, and her lips met his in a soft, yielding kiss. Rune relished the feel of her mouth, lost in her. She sucked his tongue and rocked her hips, grinding against him until Rune was a moment from pinning her beneath him.

She broke their kiss and rested her forehead against his as she slowly rocked over him. "It's been a while since you've been gentle," she said breathlessly.

"A thing to remedy," Rune said as he stood, taking her with him. He vanished his remaining clothing with a flicker of his mind and Faye wrapped her legs around his waist. She clung to him as he backed her against their bedpost. He held her up with a hand across her rear, and his other arm supported her back so the wood wouldn't abrade her soft skin.

He nuzzled her throat, taking in her scent. His night breeze through plum blossoms laced with heavy notes of her arousal. Keeping an easy rhythm proved more difficult than he anticipated. Every intimate flutter sang to his instincts. His fangs sharpened each time she raked her nails over his back as she squeezed his cock. The way she moaned and sighed his name.

When he could take no more, he nipped at the cuff decorating her ear. A permanent symbol tying her to him.

"Offer me your throat," he rasped, thrusting into her harder.

Faye immediately pulled her hair to the side and turned her head, exposing the slender column of her neck. "Harder," Faye breathed.

"Come with me."

Rune licked her pulse and did as she commanded. He chased his pleasure as Faye pleaded for his cock, begging him to come with her. Darkness, when she talked like this. Tension set through his shoulders and back. Pressure rose through his cock and Rune held Faye tighter. Fucking her harder.

He drove into her a final time and sank his fangs into her throat. Her dark exquisite blood coated his tongue as he spent deep inside of her. Faye tightened her thighs over his waist with bruising force and cried his name.

His heart thundered in his ears as Faye came around him. He couldn't breathe. Couldn't think. He phased them into bed before his knees buckled.

Rune licked his bite, drinking her slowly. Her nails glided over his scalp, adding to his euphoria. He clutched her closer, languidly thrusting into her.

"That was intense," she said, still trying to catch her breath.

Rune lifted his head, staring into her lightning-streaked midnight eyes. "You take all my desire and leave me weak."

"You better get used to it, big guy," Faye said, brushing his hair behind his ear. She tapped the cuff. "You're stuck with me for a long time."

Rune smiled his agreement. "Until the darkness drags me from you, love."

Takes place after A Trial of Lace and Bone.

Storm clouds stretched over Chaos's darkened sky as thunder echoed over the barren landscape. Faye glanced down at the stroller she spelled to float beside her and frowned. She silently reminded herself she wasn't using magic for *everything*. Pushing the stroller over the bones littering the ground would jar Kae and Ren, and the twins had grown too heavy to carry comfortably.

"I should've had Rune come with us. He could carry you both," Faye muttered to herself.

Lightning streaked across the sky, casting harsh shadows over her toddlers—who in turn kicked their legs and squealed, watching the dark, rolling clouds. They visited Uncle Morbid weekly for nearly a year. The Familiar King fawned over them, but the anxiety of her twins kidnapping remained with her. Having someone she trusted watching over them wasn't enough to ease her racing heart. She'd needed a defense anchored in intent. A tool who couldn't be fooled by a friendly face.

Familiar totems were Faye's peace. Little vessels bound with magic to retaliate against any harm meant for her son and daughter. With *deadly* ferocity.

The simple carriage, lined with soothing earth tones, hid away a mother's weapons. Nestled in between her children, were two Familiar totems shaped into baby rabbits. She'd made them to match her twin's hair color, but the opposite was curled beside each child. When they first began swapping totems, Faye had asked Rune if he exchanged them but he and Voshki said they hadn't.

Faye smoothed a strand of Kae's white hair behind her ear and mused, "Are you switching bunnies with your brother?"

Kae fell back in her seat and stared up at her as the black-haired rabbit dozing on her lap. Her glacier blue eyes were fathomless. She'd been too aware as an infant and the trait only intensified as the weeks gave way to months. She didn't coo or babble like her brother, and it wouldn't surprise Faye if she suddenly began talking. Sparrow bet Kae would skip her first words and speak in complete sentences.

"Just start with common tongue," she said, brushing Kae's pale cheek. Lightning arced through the clouds, illuminating them in purples and grays. Ren's bright eyes shifted to the sky and Faye couldn't help her grin. "Don't tell your dad you like this sky better than his. It'll break his heart."

Faye had grown accustomed to the bones littering the ground. Vertebrae cracked under her boots today as she made her way to Morbid's home. The stroller followed behind her, floating up the steps as she climbed.

Morbid's home was a tall, narrow house today. The gray cement face rose without windows. A bright pink door was centered over the landing. Through the crack of his door, Faye thought back, wondering if she'd ever seen his door closed. It swung open and Faye smiled.

"Ah, the Queen of Chaos and Darkness blesses me with a visit," Morbid bowed in a flourish and the edges of his sapphire trench coat softly scraped against the ground. He rose, stepping toward the baby carriage. "With Hell's young Prince and Princess."

Ren babbled and lifted his chubby hands as Kae blinked up at the Familiar King.

"They both just ate and should be ready for bed in about an hour," Faye said as she bent down to straighten their blanket.

Morbid pinched the edge of the stroller and wiggled it, extracting excited laughter from Ren. The Familiar King's midnight eyes met hers and he said, "Michelle's sons survived me. Your twins will as well."

Faye straightened and quirked her lip. "Don't let them play in the bones."

"I wouldn't dream of it," Morbid said with the easy humor she'd grown fond of. He took Kae in one arm and Ren in the other before vanishing the stroller. "Have a nice night with your vicious half," Morbid said as he turned into his towering home. Her twins' Familiar totems hopped over the threshold after him.

"Thank you," Faye said through the doorway. The end of Morbid's sapphire trench coat swept the steps as they faded into the shadows. She watched until they disappeared completely and closed the door. Faye pressed her hand to the distressed oak door, needing a few moments before she could step away from her children. *They were safe here*, she reminded herself.

Morbid and her magic would protect them.

Faye phased back to her bedroom in Hell and her brows came down when she was greeted by Rune's pale blue eyes. "Did I mix the nights up?" she asked, strolling toward him.

The corner of his mouth lifted into a smirk, and he held out his hand. Faye's fingertips smoothed over his palm, and he pulled her closer. His warmth welcomed her as the curves of her body pressed into the hard plains of his. Faye closed her eyes and inhaled deeply. The scent of amber and sandalwood quieted her mind while simultaneously heating her blood.

Rune's agile fingertips caressed the small of her back and his firm lips met her forehead in a gentle kiss. "Voshki has an outing planned for your evening. I will step back after we arrive and are properly shielded."

Claws whispered over Faye's awareness a moment before Voshki's voice slipped through her mind. *I bought you a dress for our date.*

Faye peered up at Rune and smiled, knowing Voshki would see it. "Did you?" she asked playfully. Nearly everything Voshki had purchased for her had been red and leather. She could only imagine what he'd want her to wear.

A lace dress appeared on their bed and Faye leaned on Rune, staring at the garment. She'd been right about the color, but it wasn't the tight leather slip she'd imagined. This haltered garment was airy and feminine. It would be a pretty spring dress if the skirt were longer. She didn't mind leaving her back exposed, but that skirt… it would barely cover her ass.

Black poured through Rune's pale blue gaze like ink through water as their gazes connected.

"I've been imagining you in that dress all day," he purred as veined, misted shadows stretched from beneath his eyes to sway over the tops of his cheekbones.

Faye leaned back in his embrace and pressed a hand to the center of his chest. "Voshki, this is a bedroom-dress."

He leaned into her, smoothing the curve of his black-tipped claw under her jaw. His fingers threaded into her hair as he caressed the sensitive skin beside her ear. "Wear this for me, vsenia," he murmured, low and soft.

A moment from her lips.

Anticipation heated Faye's blood. Her nipples tightened into hard peaks as heat bloomed between her thighs. Memories of Voshki's rough lovemaking echoed through her body. The tight grip on her hips. The way he pinned her face-down against their silk blankets. The ecstasy of his thick cock brutally thrusting into her when he was desperate to come.

"I'll wear a jacket over it," Faye said before leaning up and brushing her lips over his. He was gentle and when Faye pulled away Rune's pale gaze had returned. "How did Voshki get you to agree to let him take me on an outing?"

"It is not public, and we will renegotiate based on how the evening unfolds," Rune replied dryly.

There was reluctance in Rune's expression, a strain she recognized in the corners of his mouth. She knew he thought this was *unwise*, but she was glad the two of them were learning to cohabitate. Faye changed into the red lace Voshki purchased and twisted to look at her back in the mirror. If she stood perfectly still the skirt covered her, but she'd be indecent if she so much as took a step.

"Skirts should come to here," Faye said, tapping the tip of her middle finger to her thigh.

But your legs are stunning, Voshki argued through her mind.

Rune glanced upward and thinned his lips before strolling into her closet to retrieve her full-length winter coat.

"Are you going to tell me where we're going or is it a surprise?" Faye asked as Rune helped guide her arms into the warm fur-lined sleeves.

"I have arranged a room at Kayla's brothel for the evening. I believe Voshki feels jilted you were with me during our first two visits," Rune said with a grin.

Faye laughed, buttoning her jacket. She'd secretly wanted to go back to witness more training, but she'd been shy, and life had gotten in the way. If Kayla was as discreet as Rune said, maybe this could become a routine outing every few months. Faye bit the inside of her lip. Would Voshki want her to sit on his lap while they witnessed training? Or the bed?

She mentally shook herself and smoothed her hands over her hips. She could see why Voshki chose such a short skirt now. Satisfied the jacket would keep her covered, she turned toward Rune.

"Shall we?" Faye asked, outstretching her hand.

Their fingers intertwined and the corner of Rune's mouth lifted into the arrogant smirk she adored. Their surroundings darkened and a luxurious red room snapped into sharp focus. They were surrounded by finely crafted furniture, free standing candelabras, and freshly cut black roses meticulously curated throughout the space.

"Is this the same room we were in before?" Faye asked, wondering if her vampire had a specific room or if all the rooms were identical.

"The largest room is reserved when witnessing training," Rune explained. A knock sounded and Faye straightened suddenly, turning toward the door. Rune chuckled and smoothed his hand over the small of her back. "Nervous, vsenia?"

"No," Faye answered too quickly.

She bit the inside of her lip as a flush carried over her cheeks. In the comfort of their bedroom, she could quietly admit her desires to Rune and Voshki. Whispering her secrets when she was wrapped in their arms. She'd been brave until realization dawned on her.

Kayla would know watching a man worship at a woman's altar made her wet.

Faye pushed her insecurities away. She was allowed to want the things she desired and Voshki seemingly wanted to recreate what

Sparrow deemed as her first date with Rune.

She clung to her bravado and glanced up at her vampire. "You're concealing us before everything starts? Like last time?"

Rune lifted her hand and pressed his lips to the back of her fingers. "Kayla will enter first, then bring in one of her ladies."

Faye recalled Rune's words the first time she'd accompanied him here. *The women are not entitled to know the identity of those who service them. Kayla is the madame, she and her managers are the only ones privy to the identity of their clients.*

Faye supposed she was a client now, too.

Voshki's presence purred through her mind. *If you don't want to be here vsenia, we can leave.*

"No, this is fine," Faye said, squeezing closer to Rune. "I'm just a little nervous."

Rune smiled down at her and tucked a strand of hair behind her ear. "No one will know your predilections," he promised. "I deal with Kayla exclusively. Our secrets begin and end with her."

Rune was reserved and secretive, anyone he delt with would keep their personal life private.

"Shall we?" Rune asked. At her nod he turned toward the door. "Come in."

Kayla entered and quietly closed the door behind her. She wore a beautiful gown with an embroidered antique gold corset decorated with dozens of tiny golden chains. Her bustled skirt fell into a small train that rustled against the plush carpet as she approached.

"Queen Faye. Shadow Prince," Kayla said with a bright smile. She curtsied low and her dark curls fell forward over her bare shoulders. "It's an honor to see you again."

Faye smiled, inclining her head. "Thank you for having us."

"Of course, did you need to alter your accommodations or order refreshments before we begin?" Kayla asked.

Faye glanced up at Rune and he arched a brow at her. She smiled shakily and returned her attention to Kayla. "We have everything we need."

"Very well, I will return shortly with Mina," Kayla said before gracefully exiting the room.

Faye stepped into Rune after the door closed clicked shut. She hooked her fingers through his belt loops and took a stabilizing breath. A crimson so dark it looked black flooded his eyes as veined misted shadows swayed over the tops of his cheekbones.

"Are we invisible?" Faye asked.

"No one will see us," Voshki murmured, lifting his chin toward the dark wood canopy draped in layers of crimson silk. "Or the bed."

Voshki gazed down at his dark queen, unbuttoned her coat until the leather slipped from her shoulders. Swiftly replacing the sensation with his black tipped claws, tracing down the length of her spine. Faye drew a breath and he grinned.

"I scent you're wet," Voshki purred.

His hand dropped lower, caressing the curve of her ass. The soft curves of her body molded against his as she stepped into him. Her scent enveloped him. Sharpening his focus until all that remained was her. His night breeze through plum blossoms.

Voshki took her wrists and gently pulled them away from his belt. "It makes me hard," he groaned against her lips. "But I won't fuck you yet."

Faye stood on her toes and Voshki leaned back, maintaining their intimate distance. Her gold-streaked eyes gleamed as her lips curled into a playful smile. "Are edging me?"

The door clicked open. Voshki withheld his response as Kayla reentered, leading a tall red headed woman by the hand. Dozens of candles ignited at once throughout the space, illuminating her golden robe in a soft glow.

Voshki was indifferent to the women. His only concern was Faye and if she wanted to watch a male tongue a stranger's cunt, he would arrange it.

"Not in the way you're imagining," he said, intertwining his fingers with hers but Faye's attention was riveted to the women. Voshki chuckled and led her to the canopy bed.

His queen turned away from him as the Shadow Prince rose through his mind. Apprehension radiated off Rune, but he remained silent. *I think our queen isn't the only one who likes to watch,* Voshki said through his mind.

I see your plans for the evening. Be easy with her, the Shadow Prince warned.

Voshki helped Faye out of her coat, and she crawled onto the crimson sheets. She turned toward him momentarily to smile and continued watching the red head take a seat on the chaise decorated in gold accents.

Faye heart rate increased, and she wet her bottom lip. Voshki's lashes lowered to the plunging red lace between her breasts. The hard peaks of her nipples pressing against the thin fabric and Voshki couldn't decide if he wanted to pinch and tease her through the lace or push it aside—he loved palming her breasts while he fucked her.

Does that look like a woman who's nervous? Voshki chuckled.

The door opened and an Artithian male entered next. His platinum blonde hair was a stark contrast to the dark gray wings folded tightly toward his back.

Voshki stripped off his jacket and dress shirt, tossing them carelessly over the back of the nearest chair. He joined Faye, hooking his chin on her shoulder as he crawled behind her. He sat back on his heels and gripped Faye's hips, pulling her between his knees. The silken texture of her long dark hair was pleasant, but he needed to feel her. He smoothed the strands over one shoulder and pressed his chest to her back, trailing kisses down the side of her throat.

Faye laced her fingers with his hand on her hip. She leaned into him, arching her back until the curve of her ass ground against his hardened length. His queen instinctively reached for his hand, squeezing it as the winged male kneeled before the woman. He kissed the back of her fingers and Faye rolled her hips again. Voshki nipped the golden cuff decorating his queen's ear.

The cuff bearing *his* name.

Voshki's lips curved into an arrogant smile, and he pinned Faye's waist, keeping her from rocking her perfect ass over his cock. His free hand slid over the top of her thigh and slipped beneath her dress. He pushed the lace thong aside and carefully ran his finger through her folds.

Darkness, she was so wet.

"You like to watch," Voshki purred, gliding a second finger through her silken flesh. He moved higher, circling her clit and a trembling breath slipped past Faye's parted lips. "But you don't want to be seen."

His queen nodded, never taking her eyes from the couple on the chaise. Mina caressed the side of the male's face and smiled as she tangled her fingers through his hair.

"Artithian?" she asked.

"Yes, my lady," he answered in a voice filled with shadows.

The red head's smile brightened and she leaned back. "I could tell when you took off your shirt."

Faye squirmed against his grip, rolling her hips as he circled her clit. Once. Twice. She moaned and reached for him. Her fingers smoothed over the side of his throat and Voshki purred, closing his eyes. She cupped her hand over the back of his neck and pulled him closer.

"I want you inside me," she breathed.

Voshki's fangs ached. It would be easy to spread her legs and drive his considerable length into her wet cunt. He lingered in the moment, grazing his fangs over Faye's throat. She shivered and shifted her thighs further apart before offering him her throat.

"I can't fuck you here," he murmured, careful to keep Faye from grinding the curve of her ass against his cock. He nipped her and she went still.

Darkness, her quiet obedience made his cock hard. He exhaled and said, "The stone walls make the Shadow Prince… tense. But you could witness more training. Fuck yourself while I hold you. Give him a better memory when he sees stone walls."

Faye leaned forward and glanced at him over her shoulder. She smoothed her hand over his and pressed her lips before saying, "I'm surprised he hasn't pulled you back."

Voshki chuckled. *Our queen is concerned,* he mused through his mind only to be answered by silence. The Shadow Prince didn't need to speak when frustrated aggression radiated off him in jagged waves.

Be easy, Voshki said gently. He drew Faye closer and said, "I would have reached for your mind and told you anyway… and deep down he knows I'm right." Voshki ran his fingers through Faye's dark locks. The strands slid through his fingers, cool and soft. He leaned closer. The smooth skin of her back went flush against his chest. He'd never practiced restraint, but bringing the Shadow Prince back to her fully would please her.

Voshki lowered his voice to rasp at her ear, "After you've come to my satisfaction, I'll phase you to the gardens and fuck your pretty cunt until you scream my name, vsenia."

Her heart raced and Voshki scented her arousal. He purred as his instinct screamed to pin her to the bed and force her thighs apart. He wanted her desire to coat his tongue as he licked and worshipped her silken flesh.

Voshki breathed in her scent and called a black box. He placed the gift in front of Faye. The Shadow Prince had questioned his choice as they shopped Kayla's arsenal, and he expected Faye would as well.

His queen opened the box and stammered at the contents. She leaned back and turned her head to one side, still tangled in his arms. "What am I supposed to do with this?" Faye asked with a giggle.

"Sit on them," Voshki replied.

"There are two…" Faye lifted the grinding pad as though he hadn't purchased it.

Voshki purred as he took the heavy silicone toy from Faye and laid it flat. Its weighted base held the two smooth phallic pillars upright. The purple support faded to lavender at the base of the cocks, which in turn became pink at the tip.

"And you'll writhe on them for me," Voshki said. They weren't as thick as his own cock, and the Shadow Prince had taken her like this many times.

"Voshki," Faye hissed as blush crept over her cheeks.

Voshki took a small metal tray topped with an ornate glass container from the box. He leaned closer, brushing the curve of her ear as he spoke. "Oil them the same way you would my cock. Show me how much you want me."

The scent of Faye's arousal spiked and Voshki watched as she poured the clear liquid into her palm and fisted the first cock. Her hand slid down the shaft and back up, twisting over the head. She leaned forward, turning to meet his heated stare. Voshki's mind blanked as she smoothed the pad of her thumb over the silicone tip in a practiced motion and stroked down the shaft again.

A growl emanated from Voshki's chest. He could almost feel her, as though she were gripping his cock instead. He followed the edge of her thong to the strap over her hip and sliced through the lace with his black-tipped claw. Faye made no objections when he discarded the ruined lace.

His lips touched her throat the same moment he conjured a phantom mouth to lick and purr on her clit. Faye moaned, squeezing the second cock as she rocked her hips. Voshki ran his black tipped claws along the underside of her breast. He pinched her nipple between his thumb and forefinger before asking, "Are you aching?"

A breathless cry slipped past her sweet lips. The same sound she made when he'd bound her wrists and ankles to their bed. He'd stretched her pretty cunt around the tip of his cock while he lazily teased her breasts and used a phantom mouth on her clit.

He tugged on the hard peak, extracting a sweet cry from his panting queen. "Finish oiling that cock and bring it between your legs."

Faye did as he asked and rose up on her knees. The grinding pad was too far forward and Voshki had no intention of letting her ride one cock. She would take them both into her body, fucking her cunt and ass because it pleased him.

He snaked an arm around her waist and moved forward. Faye gasped when the toy touched the entrance to her ass. He sat back on his heels and held it in place. "Sit on them, love," Voshki purred. He kissed her hair and lifted his gaze to the Artithian male between Mina's thighs. His wings shifted as he worshipped her, licking and stroking his fingers inside her under Kayla's watchful eye. "Show me how you'd want me and the Shadow Prince to fuck you while you witness training."

Faye dropped her hips and moaned as she took the very tips into her body. She rose up, taking more of her new toy with each fall of her hips.

Voshki palmed her breast and roughened the phantom purr on her clit. He smiled as Faye cried out. She leaned forward, bracing herself on her hands while she shamelessly fucked her cunt and ass with the toy beneath her.

"That's it," Voshki rasped. He teased her nipples, plucking them between his thumb and forefinger. "Come for me, vsenia. Show the Shadow Prince how much you miss his will in your pretty cunt and ass when he fucks your throat," Voshki said caressing either side of her neck.

"Voshki," Faye panted, rocking faster over the toy beneath her.

He applied the slightest pressure to either side of Faye's neck. "Call his name and come for him, vsenia," Voshki murmured, sliding his hand to the base of her throat. "He'll hear you."

"Rune," Faye said in a broken cry. Her hips rose and fell faster. "Rune, please," she whispered as her breaths seized. She rocked harder and her hips fell a final time. She tensed, shuttering in Voshki's arms before going boneless.

She smelled different when she came. Sweeter. Voshki kissed her shoulder and leaned forward, crossing his arm in front of her, between her breasts. He took hold of her shoulder and leaned over her, placing his free hand beside hers on the bed.

"Do you like pleasing us my queen," Voshki asked. Faye moaned so sweetly as he leaned forward holding her to his chest. Her hips lifted a few inches with his movements. His lips brushed the shell of her ear as he rasped, "Having both our cocks inside you."

Faye clutched his arm when he rocked back, bringing her lower.

"You'll take us deep," he growled, lifting her again and forcing her lower each time.

Faye threw her head back, arching her back as she tensed. Voshki held her tighter, working her lithe body up and down the entire length of the cocks in her cunt and ass. Fucking her in a way the Shadow Prince could be present for without triggering his unwanted memories.

"Darkness, Voshki," Faye said in a strangled cry.

He slowed, easing his tempo. "You're not watching your couple," he teased.

Faye leaned her head back on his shoulder and he nipped the underside of her jaw. She blinked, turning toward him.

"We should have the Shadow Prince join us next time. You can witness a male at the end of his training. I think we can make you come harder and more often than the woman on the chaise."

Her pulse point flicked with each beat of her heart and Voshki leaned closer. He wanted to be inside her. Feel every intimate flutter around his cock. The scent of her arousal made his cock ache and his fangs throb. Voshki kissed the side of her neck and chuckled when she offered him her throat.

She was perfection.

Everything he'd ever dreamed of.

Voshki rubbed the side of his face against her hair in an animalistic show of affection. He kept his rhythm light and gentled the phantom mouth between Faye's thighs until she arched against him and rocked her hips.

"Ask us to fuck you harder," he purred.

Faye's breaths turned shallow as she reached behind him to fist his hair.

A low growl vibrated through Voshki. He brushed his lips over the cuff in her ear before grating, "Tell me to fuck you harder, vsenia."

"Harder," Faye whimpered. "Please."

Voshki took a vicious pace, gripping her waist and driving her up and down her toys.

"Beg for it," he growled.

She tugged on his hair as she squeezed her breast and pinched her nipple. "Please Voshki, fuck me. Rune. Harder," she cried.

Voshki lifted her off the grinder and phased them to the garden between their room and the nursery. He set her on her hands and knees in the grass and unfastened his pants.

Faye scrambled backwards suddenly and Voshki caught her as she backed into him. "What's wrong, vsenia?"

"We can't be here," Faye hissed.

Their surroundings darkened and cleared in another green space. Voshki surveyed the unoccupied rooms and the darkened archways. He glanced down at Faye as she giggled. "Was there something wrong with our garden?" he asked. He'd fucked her there dozens of times.

"No," Faye said through her laughter. "I forgot Kimber was spending the night. She sleeps in the twin's room so the beasties don't pile on her for bedtime stories. I'm just glad she was already asleep. She could have seen you," Faye said, motioning to his cock.

"She won't see anything if I'm inside you," Voshki purred. "Now, get on your hands and knees and spread your legs for me, vsenia."

Faye turned and leaned forward until her shoulders touched the lush grass. Voshki groaned as the moonlight illuminated her toned legs and the curve of her ass. The red lace of her dress fell over her back, giving him an unobstructed view of her exquisite pussy.

He needed to be inside her. Feel her cunt squeezing his cock as she came around him. Voshki fisted his cock and pressed into her wet heat. She pushed against him, taking him deeper and Voshki's lids slid closed. He gripped her hips, thrusting into her harder. She took every stroke and arched her back for more.

Voshki lost himself in her. The rhythm of her breaths, the fall of her hips, the sway of her hair, all of it intoxicated him. Each moment. Every detail.

Faye cried his name and Voshki chased his pleasure.

"Darkness save me!"

Voshki bared his fangs and stood, turning toward the intruder. He didn't care if they saw his form, but his queen—No. He would rip every memory of Faye beneath him from their mind.

Piece by piece.

Sparrow stood in the archway. Her gaze racked over his body and her mouth slacked. Faye scrambled to her feet, shoving herself in front of him.

"Voshki, stop," she said in a firm tone. He growled in answer, and she grabbed either side of his face, dragging his head down to meet her lightning-streaked midnight eyes. "Stop. It's okay," she said, nodding at him slowly as her thumb caressed his cheek.

Voshki's dark eyes rose, and a wall of shadow and ash erupted before the archway. Embers of blue hellfire glinted within the ominous swirling mass, illuminating whispers before burning out. His gaze swept over his surroundings and the same vicious magic closed off the two additional entryways.

Calm yourself, the Shadow Prince said through his mind. Voshki felt his presence rise to the surface, ready to reclaim the body they shared. *You did not secure the garden. You are more to blame than the harpy.*

As though on queue, the harpy in questions yelled, "Stop trying to kill my sister with that monstrosity. She's smaller than you, killer."

"By the Darkness," Faye muttered with a slight shake of her head before yelling over her shoulder, "Hooker, go away."

Amusement rippled from the Shadow Prince and Voshki bristled. *The blonde one saw our queen beneath me, and you think it's funny?*

I believe the harpy mentioned she has seen Faye naked more times than we have. Faye is not offended, and I believe it best to follow her lead, Rune answered before drifting into the recesses of their mind.

Faye squeezed his hand, drawing his attention. When he gazed down at her she offered him a shy smile. "You okay, big guy?"

Guilt ate at Voshki. His failure was a knife in his chest. "I'm sorry, vsenia. I didn't mean for others to see you."

She giggled and he exhaled. "This was bound to happen. You and Rune like being outside and Sparrow is nosey."

Voshki didn't correct her. Rune needed the difference in scenery to separate his memories and Voshki participated in his acclimation for Faye's sake. Every layer he incorporated to separate Faye from the bitches who enslaved them, was another step in healing the hurt their queen inflicted on herself. She wasn't responsible for the cruelty they were subjected to centuries ago, but she blamed herself all the same.

"Should I draw you a bath, love?" Voshki asked.

"A bath?" Faye teased. She ran her nails along his still-hard cock and looked up at him innocently. "I thought you said I would be screaming your name."

Voshki gripped the back of her thighs and lifted her against him, guiding her legs around his lean waist. He smiled up at her and said, "I did say that didn't I?"

Voshki phased them to Faye's private gardens in Hell. *Where he should have brought them.* Hell was an extension of himself, and he could feel they were alone in the Shadow Prince's realm. He strolled to the canopy daybed between the willow trees framing the hot spring Faye claimed as her own. He trailed kisses down the side of her neck and laid her gently on the silk draped bed.

"Hold on to the bars," he whispered to her before pulling away.

Faye turned away from him and made a show of crawling to the headboard. Voshki's fangs sharpened as she rolled her hips with each step. The short lace skirt gathering at her waist. He couldn't decide if he wanted to fuck her pretty cunt or have her sit on his face.

She leaned against the ornate iron bars and arched her back, giving him a better view. Voshki stripped out of his slacks as she glanced back at him.

Minx, Rune thought and Voshki chuckled, joining her. He grazed his black-tipped claws down her exposed back. He leaned back and pressed into her, watching her soft flesh stretch to take him.

"Voshki stop teasing me," Faye sighed. She rocked back taking several inches of his cock.

He thrusted his considerable length into her and pulled back, fucking her harder. "Spread your legs and take it, vsenia," Voshki rasped, driving into her again.

Faye moaned, parting her thighs. She pushed her hips back, meeting each of his punishing thrusts and a growl rumbled from Voshki's chest.

"You're such a good girl," Voshki groaned. His hand closed over hers on the bars. He kissed her neck, her shoulder, and kept his rhythm as he fucked her ruthlessly. Faye's breathless cries were the perfect companion to the groan of metal rattling from the bedframe.

He nipped the smooth skin between her shoulder blades. "I want to see your wings, love."

Faye's fists tightened over the wrought iron bars and two perpendicular black lines bloomed on her back. Veined misted shadows spread from the center so much like Voshki's own dark gaze. The Darkness flared from her back, arcing on either side of her. It dissipated as quickly as it arrived, leaving glittering iridescent wings in their wake.

"Come for me, Voshki. Please I need you," she cried.

"Do you?" Voshki purred.

Faye whimpered and arched her back harder, taking him. Accepting him and all he was.

Voshki's heart hammered in his ears. He took her harder, bending the wrought iron under his grip. He came with a growl and sank his fangs into Faye's throat. The beat of her heart matched his as her dark exquisite blood coated his tongue. He spent deep inside of her as Faye screamed his name. Her scent sweetened and he swallowed, taking her into himself.

Her heartbeat calmed and his followed, leaving him euphoric. He stroked the innermost part of her wing where the membrane met her back and Faye moaned, pulling them in closer.

"I meant to stroke your wings and make you come, but someone seemed impatient," Voshki said, tracing small circles along her wing.

Faye's wings became less substantial and darkened into a swirling black mist edged in purple tendrils. They dissipated completely and she said, "You've done enough to me tonight big guy." She rolled her hips and Voshki groaned. "A bath would be nice now. And maybe a snack before bed."

Voshki chuckled and licked his bite before healing it. "Yes, my queen."

Curious about our stray cat author's writing process?

Join Kalista's Patreon. Kalista's Familiar get to see each iteration of her projects as she writes them from first draft to final product.

www.patreon.com/kalista_neith

Acknowledgments

To my wonderful Muses: Kayla, Phyllica, and Kellbell. Your support allows my creativity to thrive. Thank you for taking this wild journey with me and offering your invaluable opinions on the projects and art my spicy brain fixates on. You all mean more to me than I could ever express.

To my Chaos Demon: I worship the very ground you walk on, Holy Father. I can't thank you enough for quieting my fears with these stories. Three holes or nothing. Full send! These pages are Jadussy approved.

To the Raven King: Thank you for your amazing eye and focusing my lens to terrifying clarity. You've helped me elevate these stories and stay true to the characters.

To my wildly talented narrators Corvin King and Allie Shae: You are more than I could have ever dreamed of. The way the two of you bring my characters to life will never cease to astound me. Thank you for adding dimension and life into my words.

To my Morally Grey Side Hoez: Jamie Applegate Hunter, Jeneane O'Riley, Luna Laurier, and Amber V. Nicole. I love you bitches, and we've come so far ladies. I can't wait to see what the future holds for us.

To Erin, Delaney, Rainer and the entire crew at Tempe, AZ Barnes & Noble: I will never be able to express my gratitude for your kindness and generosity. You took a chance on my stray cat ass and let me sign in your store when my first book came out. Y'all fed me tuna—and adopted me—and I'm elated to call your store my home. I love y'all and you can tell them you're my favorite store. Show them this book, lol.

To my readers: Thank you all for taking this journey with me. I can't express what it means to me. I am so grateful for each and every one of you. With all that being said, no I will not pay for the therapy you'll need after reading my books—*cackles manically*.

And finally to my war horse: Thank you for your patience and loving me through my madness. For embracing my chaos and building my gothic library. Our endearment would come a lot sooner if I was left unsupervised. I love you. Til death, baby.

About the Author

Kalista Neith
Where enemies go to fall in love...

Kalista Neith is an Amazon and Barnes and Noble best-selling dark fantasy author who writes about love. What people are willing to endure to obtain it, and what they will sacrifice to keep it.

She lives in the Phoenix area with her partner and several four-legged creatures. When she is not writing, Kalista can typically be found buried in her digital art, or playing her favorite games.

Kalista Neith can be found online at:

KalistaNeith.com
Linktr.ee/KalistaNeith

Curious about our stray cat author's writing process?
www.patreon.com/Kalista_Neith

www.ingramcontent.com/pod-product-compliance
Lightning Source LLC
Chambersburg PA
CBHW062004190726

48285CB00003BA/1200